Teaching
Training
Teasing
Sierra

BDSM Training School Parts 1-3

LEXIE RENARD
BDSM EROTICA

Welcome to my perverted little world, where sexy people love to play with sensations of pleasure, pain, submission and control. Want more?
Get on the email list for a free story!
www.LexieRenard.com

lexie.renard@gmail.com   **@lexierenard**

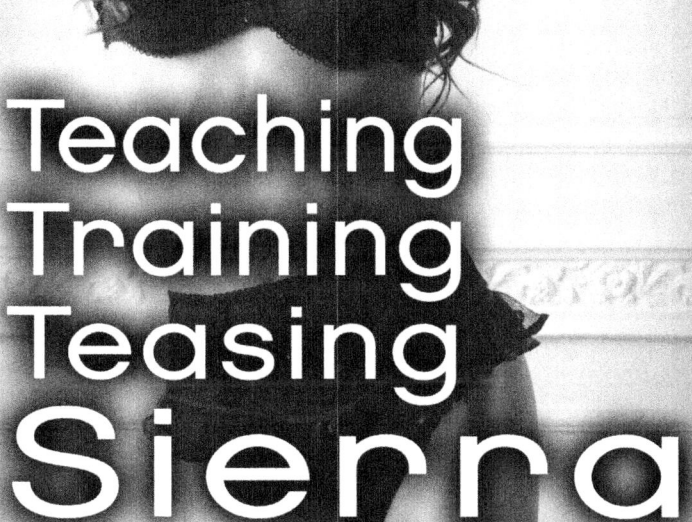

Teaching
Training
Teasing
Sierra

BDSM Training School Parts 1 - 3

LEXIE RENARD
BDSM EROTICA

***

Table of Contents

Teaching Sierra
(BDSM Training School Book #1)

*** THE BDSM ACADEMY ***

The BDSM Academy is rarely spoken of beyond a whisper. Nobody even quite knows which Dominants are a part of the group. But if you beg the owners, organizers, and Dominants of the most respected dungeons, they may pass your name along for consideration.

A few years ago, seven of the most respected Dominants and Dominatrixes in the city banded together to create a program where submissives could safely learn as much as they wanted about the BDSM world in a safe environment.

The group was tired of seeing nervous newcomers so desperate for the experience that they allowed less than reputable "Masters" and "Mistresses" to pick them up. With no experience, guidance, or mentorship, it was far too easy for abusive and manipulative people to take advantage of them.

The only problem was that there were far too many slightly curious people who were looking for a workshop or two. Those were already available every few weeks at other venues.

In order to sign up for the BDSM Academy, applicants would have to commit to a thirty day, twenty-four-seven submissive lifestyle, giving themselves completely to the whim of their Master or Mistress. This would ensure that they were extremely serious. It would allow them to completely fall into the submissive headspace, learn about the lifestyle, but more importantly, discover what they really wanted for themselves.

One can only determine what one truly needs from a Dominant if one has been dominated.

This program was setting new people up with the skills they would need to go on to find healthy relationships and be better able to communicate their needs.

The seven Dominants who made up the group were able to expand their own skills and styles with these new submissives, while imparting their wisdom, and strengthening the community at large.

It was also a delight to play with new subs, facilitate their training, and watch them grow. At their monthly events, there would be a large group of regulars who were eager to play with the new recruits.

But first, the brand new submissives would have to survive the first day.

*** SIERRA'S FIRST SPANKING ***

A soft blindfold was secured over my eyes, and I felt a chill run through me as his fingers caressed the nape of my neck. He gently pulled back my long auburn hair, working it through a ponytail holder with practiced hands while I tried to remain still as a stone. I was always extremely nervous around attractive men, so perhaps not being able to stare at his gorgeous face and hypnotic dark eyes would help me attempt to stay calm.

A thick leather collar was buckled around my throat, and he gave it a little shake just to let me know that my body was now his.

He unbuttoned my shirt, letting it fall to the floor. Unhooking my bra, it was almost as if he were unwrapping a package that he wasn't quite sure he was interested in. His movements were deft, mechanical. But then as he let my bra tip forward, revealing my small but firm breasts, I felt him pause.

His thumb ran along the inside curve of my skin, then he glided his hand out to lightly pinch my nipple. I tried so hard not to have a reaction, but as he pinched again, much more firmly, I couldn't help but release a tiny gasp.

"There it is," his low voice growled, practically in my ear. He went back to removing my clothing, tossing my bra aside, unzipping my skirt, and guiding it over my slim hips. I didn't have the most womanly figure, but I was petite and toned, with just enough curves. Even though I was completely his captive, I wanted him to want me. I needed him to desire me.

Hooking his thumbs into the sides of my panties, he pulled downward slowly, revealing my naked sex. I felt myself blushing ferociously, and was thankful for the blindfold. There was no way I could have met his eyes at that moment.

He took a step away from me, and I wondered if he was examining me, to decide what positions in the house would be suited to a new slave like me.

"Such a tiny little thing," he murmured to himself. "So delicate. I might have to toughen you up the old-fashioned way."

Standing perfectly still, my arms at my sides, I could feel my nipples harden as if threatening to jump away. My stomach was clenched, and my thighs pressed together.

"You are aroused," he said flatly. I wasn't sure whether or not I was supposed to answer, so I remained silent.

"I think you are going to enjoy this, Sierra," his low, throaty voice insisted. "All you have to do is let go. Your body is now mine. You belong to my house. You exist only to serve. Isn't that refreshing?"

"Yes, Sir," I whispered.

"Won't you feel perfect fulfillment when you are serving me every day for the next month?"

"Yes, Sir," I whispered again. I wasn't sure if I believed it, but it was too late now.

His hand settled on the top of my shoulder, and I flinched involuntarily. "Poor little sparrow," he said softly. "You are going to be touched a lot during your time here. You will have to become accustomed to it."

I nodded very slightly. He set his hand on the small of my back, and I almost gasped.

"Do you not like being touched?"

"It's fine, Sir," I breathed.

"Are you always this jumpy?" he asked, and it almost sounded as if he were smiling.

"I startle easily, especially when I'm nervous, Sir."

"Good girl. Continue being honest, and everything will be easier for you."

He took my hand, guiding me forward. He sat on the bed, pulling me so that I was standing between his legs.

I felt the crisp fabric of his suit brushing my hips, and realized I had no idea whether or not he would want to have sex with me during this first night in his home. I sort of assumed that he might want to take his time, or train me first, but he seemed to be throwing me in the deep end right away.

His hands lightly cupped my backside, pulling me against him. "Put your arms around my neck, my little sparrow," he whispered, and I obeyed immediately.

His lips met mine, and I gasped in surprise, but pressed back against him immediately. His mouth was softer than I would have expected, as I opened my lips slightly, inviting him in. The tip of his tongue ran along my bottom lip, almost making me giggle, then he entered my mouth, gently exploring as his huge thick fingers pressed against my rear, pulling me closer.

I felt my nerves fluttering, completely enchanted by the way he kissed me so deeply, so confidently. I genuinely felt like his toy, and it was positively enthralling.

He pulled back, very gently, moving his lips to my ear as he breathed, "I adore the way you kiss, little girl."

I felt my lips quirk up in an automatic tiny smile. The thought that I had pleased him was rewarding.

"You know that part of your training will require punishment and reward," he said. "Now is the time I must demonstrate one of our punishments so that you can understand your place."

He pushed me away, causing me to step back so that he could pull his knees together, then he threw me over his lap as if I were a doll. His hand brushed firmly over my rear, and I knew what was coming. Surely he'd be gentle on my very first day.

"Now is the time for you to tell me precisely why you're here," he said sternly. "Why did you sign your life away for the month to join this house?"

"I… I wish to learn discipline, Sir," I said gently.

The palm of his massive hand struck the outside of my butt cheek in a firm, stinging blow. I squealed, unable to maintain my composure.

"Why are you at my house?" he said again, his gravelly tone more firm.

"I want to learn my limits, Sir, and find out more about myself so that I can be less nervous all the time."

This time it was three harsh spanks, each one stinging more than the last until my eyes burned with tears as much as my skin burned from the hard slaps. But there was also a burning between my legs, as he touched me with such confidence and power.

"Why did you come to my mansion?" he demanded.

"I…" I felt something inside me break. Some portion of my mind disintegrated, and the fear of admitting my desires was not as bad as me not confessing them.

I felt his hand draw back again, and quickly blurted, "I've always dreamed of being a man's sexual toy. I've hardly ever had sex, but I desperately need to. I'm afraid that I'm not good at it. I want to man to teach me, I want to be his plaything and have him use me any way he likes."

His hand came down to my burning cheek gently, caressing my skin, diminishing the pain.

Then he stood me up, pulling me against his chest, holding me while I cried softly, tiny and naked in his arms. "That's my girl. That's what I need to know." His strong hands pressed between my shoulder blades and at the small of my back, making me feel cared for and safe for the first time in my life.

"Good girl, Sierra. We will give you everything you want, you will get everything you need, and you'll be our girl this month."

I pulled myself together, swallowing hard as I forced my tears to stop. He gently pulled the blindfold off, and I was rewarded with a stunning smile from the dark, handsome stranger I had only met three days ago.

*** JEREMY'S NEW SUBMISSIVE ***

I had known from the moment I saw her in the lobby that she was going to be special. The poor thing must have used every drop of her courage to apply for admission and to actually show up at Damian's house for the interview. As always, I had been watching through the one way glass along with a few other Dominants as my assistant and submissive Paige had gone through the usual list of questions.

Applicants are always given a detailed set of forms, describing what they like, what they absolutely will not do, and what they are curious about. There are usually a few things that people say they would never do, but would like to watch. This is why we sometimes make them retake the survey after a week or two. It's amazing how your reaction to watching something will allow you to admit that you're secretly enthralled, and can't wait to try it yourself.

Sierra had filled out all of the paperwork and answered every question perfectly, but her primary reason for signing up had been the only answer I didn't quite believe.

When regular women want discipline, they join the army or take a hardcore fitness class. Giving your life to another for a full month was a level of servitude that was not normal, or even logical. For a woman to do this, there must be real, deeper reasons.

So my scared little bird didn't think she was sexually experienced enough. I could feel her skin practically glowing when I touched her. The sensuality came off her in waves. All she needed was confidence and encouragement, which I could certainly provide.

But also giving her structure, and taking the control and decisions away from her would help her to let go. If one is obeying commands, nothing that happens is their fault. She's not a dirty girl, her obedience in doing dirty things makes her a good girl.

I was extremely fortunate to be part of this collective, and that I worked from of my giant home so that it was easy for me to have several submissives stay here. Luckily, it was my turn to have the first pick of this round of potentials, and Sierra was my selection. She was totally mine for the next thirty days, to play with, to train, to encourage.

Oh, I was going to have fun with this sweet thing. Hopefully not too much fun though. With a woman this beautiful, this naturally submissive, it was hard for me to keep my guard up, but I could not get too attached. I really didn't wish to take on another permanent house pet right now, unless we were truly meant to be.

Sierra also seemed to understand the system of fines should she leave early. Submissives are free to leave at any time, but it must be a serious decision. They can't give up in a moment of weakness. Some people are so used to taking the easy way out these days. An expensive fine nearly always makes them rethink everything, and they continue on, blasting through their mental blocks along the way.

She wanted to challenge herself, but I don't think she had enough grounding to make her decisions stick without a little help.

After our preliminary bonding session, I sent Sierra into the care of Chloe, my house pet. It would make her feel better to know all of the basics, such as where her room was, the washroom, shower, and kitchen. She would be told all of the rules regarding food, bedtime, and behavior when she was left on her own.

Chloe has been my domestic pet and submissive for years, and she has been an absolute dream to be with, especially her help with training newbies. I may have taken her as my personal submissive, however, we are not sexually compatible. As much as she loves to be dominated by men, she cannot bear the thought of becoming sexual with one.

This is fine, and we do share hugs and cuddles after her occasional punishments. But she spends her weekends with her girlfriend who lives on the other side of town.

I have never found a personal submissive that really clicked with me completely, yet I tried not to actively search for one. These things should happen naturally, accidentally. When the student is ready, the teacher shall appear, so they say. I believe the same is true with love, but also with intense sexual relationships. The spark must be unprovoked.

I definitely felt a spark when I kissed Sierra. The sort of spark that begins a forest fire that alters history. A girl that timid, but with the mental fortitude to push herself enough to try was admirable. I was genuinely curious what the next several weeks would hold.

*** SIERRA'S NEW WORLD ***

My life had been stagnant and strange for so long that I wondered if it were depression. After some careful study, I realized that I wasn't close with my friends anymore, and I was denying myself things that I was craving on a deep, primal level.

Just because my desires aren't something that I could tell my coworkers or friends about doesn't mean that they're wrong.

I made some new friends in the BDSM scene, and Master Gregory seemed to know precisely what I needed. He brought me the application for the academy, and gently encouraged me to surrender myself for the thirty-day program.

He said the only way to completely know what I needed was to give myself to an expert, and let them mold me. Through the process of servitude, I would draw sharper lines and conclusions.

It sounded very logical, but as I was being led around my new temporary home, I was extremely skittish.

"Relax," Chloe said gently. "Master will never give you more punishment than you can take. And he won't change the rules or try to trick you like some guys."

"Will, um…" I couldn't even ask I was so tied up in knots.

Chloe grinned. "Will he have you serve him in all possible ways? Yes. And you'll love it. I promise."

She led me down the hallway, showing me the washroom, the kitchen, then through a back hall. "This is your room," she said, opening the door.

It looked like a servant's quarters, with a small bed, dresser, table, and lamp. I saw that my single suitcase was already sitting on the bed. Bare bones, except for the stack of BDSM theory and technique books stacked up on the end of the dresser.

"Master prefers that we're naked as much as possible, but your collar stays on except for bathing. He would like us to read at least an hour before bed each day," she said. "He likes us to be well informed. If you have any questions, I'm next door. Be up at seven, stretch, shower, and breakfast is at seven-thirty. Master will likely call for you shortly after."

"Thank you."

I wondered how many girls had been through this. How many he had trained, or used as his plaything. I wondered if I could be good enough for him.

The feelings that rose up inside me when he had his hands on me… I couldn't understand the intensity of it all. It was too much to process, but I knew I needed much more.

I stretched, did some reading, and went to sleep early. I couldn't help wishing that I was sleeping in Master's bed with him. Those thick arms around me made me excited, calm, grounded... and more desperately aroused than I had ever been in my entire life.

*** MASTER PLAYS WITH HIS TOY ***

Although I had trained many girls, I didn't play with them all sexually. Some I teased, some I would train for blow jobs and hand jobs only. But I didn't fuck a girl unless there was a real connection, and I could tell she needed it on a deep level.

Sierra needed it. Her desire was almost visible, a halo of lust surrounding her.

But the nervous little thing was afraid to admit it to herself, and let go. Some schools of thought said to take her immediately, let her loosen up and enjoy the rest of her stay. Some experts suggested starting things slowly, to let her become accustomed to these new sensations.

I was torn.

Perhaps the kindest thing I could do was to serve her needs for the first few days, until she became more comfortable with her own sexuality, before she became all tangled up in mine.

I knew that I could be physically intimidating to tiny girls, who were used to big men being loud, rough, unpredictable. It would take some time before she knew that I was a sensualist, not a violent man.

When I called for her to meet me in the main dungeon, she tapped on the door, then entered with her head down, closing the door before stepping farther inside and dropping to her knees, exactly as instructed.

She was wearing her thick leather collar and nothing else. I was extremely glad she was open to my preferred uniform. Sometimes it took girls a few weeks to loosen up.

"Have you settled in, little one?"

"Yes, Sir."

"And have you thought about what you confessed to me last night?"

"Yes, Sir."

"Up."

She stood up immediately, standing with her head down and her wrists clasped behind her back.

Sierra was such a natural submissive that I felt myself becoming even more aroused than I already was by admiring her perky round breasts.

I pulled her against me, with my fingers against the side of her throat. Sure enough, her pulse increased steadily as she pressed against me.

"Sierra, you understand that although I shall teach you and train you this month, you are also my toy. You are here to please me."

Her heart hammered and her pupils dilated. "Yes, Sir."

"You understand your safe words, and you may use them at any time. Also, even if I have instructed you to be silent, you speak up if there is ever a problem, okay?"

"Yes, Sir."

I knew that I should start by teaching her perfect poise, how to study her Master's wishes and all of the protocol she should have burned into her, but my hand cupped her chin, tilting her mouth to mine. Our lips met softly, and the way she instantly pressed closer against me made me feel like she truly wanted me, not just this experience.

It was a rare treasure to find a girl that kisses just like you do. We fused together, her arms wrapping around my neck, and I didn't even realize I had carried her to the huge leather couch, setting her in my lap.

She opened her lips for me, allowing my tongue to explore her soft mouth. Having a woman this gorgeous in my arms was having its effect on me, and I knew she could feel it.

"Master," she whispered, "Do you… um, need me to serve you now?" She was shaking like a leaf, her eyes tight but determined.

"No, my nervous little sparrow. You're going to give

yourself to me now."

It was obvious that she didn't understand what I meant. Stroking the flower petal soft skin between her shoulder blades, I asked, "Whose body is this?"

She bit her bottom lip for half a second before answering, "Yours, Master."

Kissing the top of her shoulder, then along her throat, she gasped.

"You're surprised when I'm gentle. Why?"

"I... I just assumed that a man who spanks girls would be rough. Sir," she added quickly, but I raised my eyebrow at the pause.

"There are so many ways we can enjoy each other, little one. My power comes from control, and taking ownership of you. Your power comes from the freedom of giving yourself to me."

She nodded, but I knew it often took a while for someone to truly understand.

"This is my arm," I said, picking her arm up and giving it a little shake. "If you disobey, I might smack it, bite it, or wrap it up tight in restraints. However, if you are my perfect little doll, I might smack it, bite it, or restrain it simply to give myself pleasure."

Lifting her arm so that the inside of her elbow was at my lips, I said, "This is mine to play with however I see fit. If I choose to give you pleasure, it also pleases me." I gave her delicate skin an open-mouthed kiss, almost sucking gently as she gasped, quivering. Once her skin was slightly moist, I blew across it gently, the breeze chilling her. She shuddered as if she felt it up her spine.

"Playing with you, exploring your body, gives me great pleasure," I said gently. "You are impossibly beautiful, Sierra. But you also have such a warm, gentle energy around you that I wish to share."

Setting her arm down, I kept one hand in the center of

her back to steady her on my lap, and ran the other along her cheek, down her throat, to cup her breast.

She leaned in, not pulling away, to my great relief.

I never quite trusted new submissives to use their safewords or speak up, so I studied their body language, and other tiny visual cues to continually make sure they were okay with everything that we were doing. If I was ever in doubt, I checked in with them. Communication was the most important part of power play, and it was difficult when people were intimidated.

But Sierra's entire body was surging toward mine as I caressed her soft breast, running my thumb lightly along the nipple. Her arms were around my neck, and I felt her fingers slide up, stroking the back of my hairline.

Kissing her again with that luscious intensity, I felt her hips squirm slightly. Instantly I knew how I needed her to please me.

Sitting back farther against the couch, I pulled her so that she was sitting between my legs, facing away from me. I spread my legs wide, pulling hers out against mine.

I knew this position would make her feel open and vulnerable, but being pressed back against my chest should give her comfort. Pulling her to the right so that she could look up at me, I kissed her forehead.

Running my hands from her knees along the inside of her thighs, I pulled her tightly against me, loving the way her back rubbed up against me like a kitten about to purr. My fingertips reached higher, slowly meandering into her soft folds, exploring her most delicate skin. She leaned back completely with a deep sigh.

"Nobody has ever been gentle with you, have they, sweetheart?" Her doe eyes looked up at me in horror, but she shook her head. "I won't ask further today, sweetheart." She looked instantly relieved.

Then she gasped as my fingers skimmed along her outer

folds, tracing every curve of skin. "Your soft, sweet pussy feels lovely against my fingers," I whispered in her ear. I could feel the tremor that ran through her, especially where her tight round ass was snug up against my cock. But I tried to keep that under control for now, not wanting to frighten her.

My fingers glided between her inner lips, opening her slowly as her lips parted in a silent sigh. As my finger pressed inside her snug pussy, I brought my other hand up to squeeze her breasts firmly, back and forth.

Once I was an inch inside, I could feel how wet she was becoming. "Good girl, Sierra," I whispered into her ear. "Let yourself go. Let your lovely pussy drip for me."

"Oh," she moaned as my finger sunk as deep as it could go, while I pinched her nipple gently.

I could feel the primal part of my mind begging to throw her onto her knees and fuck her hard, but I needed to open her mind first. Lowering my other hand again, both of my arms were wrapped around her as I worked one finger in and out slowly, while tentatively circling her clit with two fingers.

"Sierra, when you pleasure yourself, do you like it soft or hard?"

"I…" she hesitated.

"Little one, you are mine. Your body is mine. I expect all questions to be answered quickly and honestly."

She nodded, the back of her silky hair pressing against my shirt. "Gentle like this, but harder if… if you were…"

"If I were fucking you?"

"Yes, Sir."

I could feel how difficult it was for her to talk of anything sexual, and vowed to help her with this. But first, I needed to feel her lose herself.

"Open your mouth."

She obeyed immediately, as I brought my fingers to her

lips, stroking them along her tongue. Lowering them back down, I circled her swollen clit softly, while sliding a second finger deep inside her with my other hand.

"Oh, oh…" her little cries were a shot of adrenaline to my already overloaded arousal. Her hands flew over her head to reach behind my neck, holding on while her body writhed. With her back arched so prettily, her breasts thrust out, nipples at attention, I could have studied her for days. She seemed to need more, but I kept my pace slow and steady, letting the tension within her build.

"My gorgeous girl, let yourself go for me. Let Master watch you come." Her eyes flew wide, and she looked up to me. I nodded. "Be my good girl now."

"Yes, Master," she whispered, with the slightest hint of a smile playing on her lips.

Shifting my arm down, I plunged two fingers into her harder, deeper, her tight, wet pussy clinging to me with each stroke. Her hands gripped my neck and hair tightly as she shifted and wiggled against me. Circling her clit carefully, I could feel her begin to quiver.

Her hips tightened, jerking back against me, her spine arching farther as her head flew back against my chest. Turning to me over her shoulder, her eyes were wild. "Kiss me," she begged, and as our lips met, her entire body spasmed, convulsing in orgasm as she squealed into my mouth.

The sensation of her tight passage pulsing against my fingers was nearly too much to take, and I couldn't wait to feel that more intensely.

She didn't stop kissing me, wiggling slowly in my arms. Jumping up, she turned in a flash, straddling me so that she could wind her arms around my shoulders, devouring my lips.

Her naked mound was pressing hard against my erection, rubbing me firmly through my pants. Caressing her back and shoulders gently, I tried to pull myself together. I had planned on pleasing her all day long, turning her into a little puddle, exhausted and spent, then having her share her desires with me.

But as much as I was a Master, given the task of training this darling girl, I was also a man with extreme needs that had not been met in several weeks.

"Fuck me, Master," she whispered into my ear. "Please. Take me."

I grabbed the back of her hand, almost roughly, holding her face in front of mine. "Are you giving your Master an order, little pet?"

"No… I…" Her breath was halted, her breasts were heaving, and it was painfully obvious that she needed it even more than I did. "I wish to serve you, Master, if you'd enjoy that."

I gripped her waist while I stood up, lowering her to her knees. She waited silently as I took my shirt off, but then her hands reached up to unbuckle my belt. There were so many details she would learn in her training, but I didn't have the heart to correct her now when her focus was on pleasing me.

Pulling off my belt, she unfastened my pants, pulling them and my shorts down. Her little gasp amused me greatly.

"Something wrong, little one?"

"I don't know if… Master… I'll try."

I knew that I was quite well endowed, but I haven't met a girl yet who couldn't take me if she were relaxed and determined. Sierra was also so wet already.

"Up."

The second she was on her feet I roughly pulled her against me, kissing her hard and deep with one hand between her shoulder blades. There was no tension. She wanted it rough. She enjoyed it when I shoved her around a bit.

Picking her up and laying her on the couch, I laid over her while kissing her throat. Placing one of her slim, pale legs over the backrest, I leaned back to admire her delicate pink pussy, so open and ready. Her glistening slit was just begging to be filled, and her eyes flashed with desperation.

"Baby girl, tomorrow I'm going to lick that perfect little twat until you scream so hard you lose your voice." Her mouth fell open in shock. "But right now, I need to make you mine."

She nodded eagerly, reaching for my thick shaft and stroking firmly. I never let a submissive take the lead, but I felt like she needed to feel a bit of control until she knew that she could fit me, and until she lost control of herself.

*** SIERRA PLEASES HER MASTER ***

I felt like my mind had completely dissolved. Wrapping my fingers firmly around his enormous, hard cock, I pulled him toward me. I knew that I was still gushing from that incredible climax, but could something this big fit inside me?

I had to try. I needed to please him. I needed him to want me more than he'd ever wanted anyone before. My spine was twitching with raw need as I guided his thick head between my inner lips.

He lowered himself slowly, and I was touched by how tender he was. But the flashing light in his dark eyes showed me how much he truly wanted to possess me.

As he began to enter me, I nearly cried in bliss. I'd never had a man be gentle with me, listen to me, watch my body for clues as Master obviously did. Although I barely knew him, I knew I needed him to teach me everything.

Gliding inside me just an inch, my body naturally opened for him.

"Good girl. Slowly now," he murmured, kissing my throat as he pressed just a touch deeper.

My arms gripped his shoulders as my hips tilted up. "Yes," I heard myself gasp. He was almost three inches inside me, taking tiny, tentative strokes. I was thankful for his self-control as he opened me.

"Sierra, my sweet girl, you feel so perfect," he murmured. Looking straight into my eyes, he pressed deeper, deeper, as we moved together. It was the most intimate moment I'd ever shared with anyone, as he filled me more, then more.

"Oh!" I gasped as I felt him brush against the very end of my tunnel. Pulling out all the way, he slowly filled me completely again, still staring directly into my eyes.

I felt nerves firing that I was never aware of before. I

felt something in my mind snap. I was floating, weightless, as he took long, full strokes into my tight, wet pussy.

"Does this please you, Master?" I whispered without thinking.

"Yes, very much." His voice sounded deeper, his throat tight. "You're so beautiful, my darling. So sexy."

Every time he filled me I thought I might explode from the overload of bliss. My hips were squirming up against him, trying to pull him deeper.

"What is it, baby? Tell me what you want, what you need."

"I hope that my gorgeous Master is enjoying me, Sir."

His hand slid under me, gripping my ass tightly. "Yes, little one. Very much." His eyebrow quirked up. "I think my shy baby girl needs to speak up more."

He pulled out so that just the tip of his cock was inside me, then stopped moving. "Darling, you'll learn that you must be silent sometimes, and extremely vocal other times, at your Master's command. For the next minute, I need you to tell me everything you feel. Start now."

As he pressed into me slowly, I moaned. "You feel amazing. I've never felt like this before."

"Like what? Keep talking or I'll stop."

"Like… like you need me to feel as much as you do. That you truly care about my desires."

He began thrusting a little faster. "Oh, Master, please… I want to be the best pet you've ever had. I want you to fuck me as much as you need. I want you to own me completely."

I stopped to breathe, and he stopped moving, except to shift his hips so that he was pressed tighter against my clit. "Please… don't stop. You feel so thick and perfect inside me. It's almost too full, the pressure is wild. It's so intense I don't want you to ever stop."

He stopped again, and I couldn't think of what else to say, as my mental control checked out completely. "Please don't stop, Master, please. I'll do anything. If you keep fucking me like this I'm going to come. Please make me come for you." His pace quickened, and I could feel his energy shift. His long, deep strokes became less gentle. As much as I loved it when he touched me softly, it was even more intense when he was rough.

"Yes, please, take me hard. Harder. Oh… fuck me so hard it hurts. Please, Master, use me, come inside me. I'm going to… oh fuck… oh please… oh Master yes!" I wailed, coming ferociously, my pussy clenching down around his thickness so hard he groaned.

"Good girl," he murmured, kissing me as I climaxed, the fiery waves engulfing me as his passion surged, fucking me harder, deeper, faster. Some primal force seemed to overtake him and I couldn't believe how incredible it felt as he pounded me harshly.

Finally his hips tightened, his cock surging inside me savagely as he filled me with burst after burst of thick, hot cum as he pounded me deeply. "Yes, Master," I moaned, gripping his shoulders, breathing him in.

He kissed me hungrily as he held me, his pace finally slowing. Rolling so that I was on top of him, I was shocked when he began to laugh.

"Sir?"

"Shh," he said as he rubbed my back. "My timid little sparrow. I knew you'd be a firecracker once you shook yourself out of your head."

I giggled, glad that it was okay to be light with him as well as intense.

He looked up at me curiously. "It was very difficult for you to keep speaking, wasn't it?"

"Yes, Sir."

"We're going to work on that."

I nodded, not sure what else to say.

"How do you feel, baby?"

I grinned. "Wow. Um, like a weight has been lifted, sort of."

"Good. What else?"

"Like..." I didn't know how honest I should be, but this month was about honesty and I couldn't help it. "Like I really belong to you now. Even though I don't know you."

"Good girl. Yes, you're mine, and you'll get to know me. You're my precious pet, and I'll be taking special care of you." He wrapped his arms around me, rocking me gently, and I was ashamed that I burst into tears.

"That's good," he said, petting my hair. "Let it all go. Nobody has taken proper care of you before, and that's what you truly need. That's okay, baby. I'm so glad you ended up here so that I can give you everything you need."

"But," I sniffled. "I thought this was about me serving you?"

"It works both ways. You'll see. For now, just keep being as open and honest and vocal as you possibly can, okay?"

"Okay."

He tipped my head up, wiping away my tears. "There's something else you want to know. What is it?"

The way he half read my mind was eerie. Swallowing hard, I blurted, "I hope that I pleased you. I hope that felt as good for you as it did for me, Master."

He sat up, pulling me against him. "Sierra, if we were only talking about physical body parts, you have the silkiest, snuggest, most luscious pussy I've ever experienced." I felt myself blushing furiously. "But sweetheart, the moment when you let go completely, offering yourself to me so openly… that was a gift. A treasure. Watching you surrender yourself was a thrill I'll never forget."

As he cuddled me, kissing my forehead, I realized that I'd never felt so special, sexy, and treasured in my life. Choking back the fresh round of tears, I vowed to become an excellent submissive for him. For both of us.

*** Master Teaches a Lesson ***

It was obvious that Sierra had a troubled past. She jumped when she was first touched, even lightly. She had trouble stating what she wanted. She was so nervous about being good enough. I didn't want to be her psychologist, I wanted to be her healer. But more than that, I wanted to be her Master, her man.

I sent her back to her room to take a nap, reassuring her that I'd call for her again after dinner. But then I realized that all I wanted for dinner was her.

Around seven I called for her, asking Chloe to send her to my bedroom. As soon as she arrived, I took a moment to admire her, deliciously naked and ready for anything. I snapped my fingers, pointing to the enormous bed. She climbed up, not sure what to do next.

"Lie on your back."

She spread out, looking so delicate across the black sheet. I quickly pulled out the restraints - thick leather cuffs that were chained to the center of the headboard. Although I loved having girls spread-eagled, I often changed my mind and wanted to flip them. Sierra didn't seem to mind the restraints at all, letting herself become my captive easily.

From under the bed, I pulled out a steel bar with leather straps on each end. Her eyes grew wide.

"Are you nervous?"

"No, Sir, just curious."

Strapping one end around each thigh just above the knee, I adjusted the bar so that her legs were spread wide, but comfortably. Then I stood on the bed, pulling two hooks down from the ceiling, attaching them to the straps so that her ass was lifted just an inch.

Placing my hand on her stomach, I pressed into her skin a little, giving her a shake. "How do you feel, pet?"

Her nipples were tight little peaks, and her pupils were

huge. "Excited, Sir."

"What do you think I might do to you, trussed up like a prize?"

"I… I assume you will fuck me, Sir. Use me for your pleasure." She was obviously delighted by the thought.

I leaned over her, kissing her gently. "There are so many lessons I must teach you, and this one might be difficult, my darling."

She nodded, waiting.

"Sometimes a submissive gets what they need, not what they want." She bit her bottom lip. "You're trying to figure out what I'm talking about." She nodded.

"Sweetheart, today I gave you what you wanted because I couldn't resist you. Now I must give you what you need, for your own good."

Sierra looked so confused, but nodded. "Whatever pleases you, Master."

"Have you ever pleasured yourself in front of someone else?"

Her head shook quickly. "No."

"No, what?"

Gasp. "No, Sir. I'm sorry, Sir."

"Thinking about touching yourself in front of someone disturbs you. Why?"

"It's so intimate. I don't… I don't think I even could."

"Which is why we're going to break that door down. The more limits you smash immediately, the farther we'll get."

She nodded reluctantly.

Standing up, I slowly took my clothing off, watching her stare at me. It was worth every lousy harsh workout to watch a woman's eyes light up when I took my shirt off. Sierra looked like she was positively starving for me, which made what I was about to do even nastier.

Staring at her soft pink pussy spread open for me, I

suddenly lunged, lapping at her hard, adoring every little moan and gasp. I knew that if I kept at it for just a few moments, she would have a gigantic climax, which would be thrilling to me as well, but I needed to begin teaching her real lessons.

Her fresh, slightly salty scent was intoxicating, and I flattened my tongue, licking up her inner lips several times before latching onto her clit.

Her entire body began to quiver with pure raw need, so I stopped, sitting back, stroking her dangling calf.

"Master?" she gasped. "Please don't stop."

"Why do you want me to continue, darling?"

"I need…"

"Say it."

"I need to come. Please, Sir," she whispered.

"I'm sorry, my sweet girl, but this is where you need to learn that your body is for my amusement, not yours."

I stood up, reaching into the drawer of the bedside table. Taking out a cuff that was on a long slim chain, I asked, "Are you right handed?"

"Yes." She looked so confused that it was difficult not to laugh.

Uncuffing her right hand from the headboard, I put it in the new cuff, fastening the ends carefully at the clips in the headboard and under the foot of the bed so that her hand was positioned directly on top of her desperate twat.

Her eyes grew wide. "You expect me to just… that?"

"Yes. Trust me, it's good for you to please yourself for my amusement." I sat at the foot of the bed, watching her hand remain motionless. "I thought you said you needed to come?"

"But… Master… I don't think I can."

"Okay. You can stay there until you climax. I'll wait," I smiled warmly.

She grinned, thinking I was kidding.

"Paige, enter," I called.

My administrative assistant and house submissive Paige entered with her head down, naked but for her collar, dropping to her knees before me, silent as a ghost.

"Sierra, this is Paige. She works for me, and occasionally I use her lovely body for my own pleasure. But if I request it, she will do anything for me."

Sierra was positively staring, while Paige was perfectly calm. She had helped me train many, many girls, and although we didn't play together often, she was always up for absolutely anything.

"Paige, lie beside Sierra and spread your pussy open for me."

She obeyed immediately, her long blonde hair flowing out behind her as she laid down, folding her hands over her stomach. I noticed that Sierra's eyes danced along her small, firm breasts, her naked mound, her long legs.

"Paige, stroke your lovely little clit until you're quite wet."

"Yes, Master," she breathed, her fingers stroking her whole twat for a moment for my obvious amusement before settling on her clit.

"See how she pleases herself to please me?" I said to Sierra. "I could sit here and do my paperwork while she came over and over for my entertainment."

My poor little pet's eyes were wide. "You've never been naked with another woman before?"

"No, Sir."

"Does this shock you?"

"I… don't know. It's strange, Sir."

Paige has always been an exhibitionist, and adored women, so it didn't take long before she was quite wet and ready.

"Sierra, good girls who obey their Masters get fucked. Have you been playing with yourself yet?"

"No, Sir." Her lips pursed, and she tentatively ran a finger over her clit.

Reaching out, I plunged two fingers inside her, fucking her roughly for just a moment. "Oh," she gasped softly, but her hand didn't move. When I pulled my fingers out, the frustration in her eyes was almost heartbreaking.

Paige's breath increased, and her nipples became rosy. I leaned over to her, pulling one into my mouth while Sierra stared. She was obviously completely aroused, but still too shy to move her hand.

I moved between Paige's legs, pulling her ass toward me roughly as she laid right beside Sierra. She was still brushing her fingers over her clit as I dipped the head of my hard cock between her wet pussy lips.

Both girls gasped. Paige closed her eyes for a moment as I pressed slowly, deeply inside her. My gaze met Sierra's wild eyes, and I blew her a kiss. She looked freaked out for just a second, then watched my shaft disappear and reappear from Paige's wet twat.

Plunging in and out of a sexy girl while another one watches, transfixed, is a slight fetish of mine that always made my blood boil.

Paige's moans grew louder, and it was obvious that she was on the edge. "May I come for you, Master?" she breathed.

"That's up to Sierra," I said. Both girls looked at me curiously. "You are only allowed to stroke your clit while I am moving inside you. I will only move if Sierra keeps talking."

Pulling out, I rested my thick head between Paige's twitching pussy lips, and she whined, quivering with need.

"Sierra, you need to keep talking nonstop about everything you see and feel. No mental filter. Let everything go, so that Paige can let go. Ready?"

She nodded, staring at the two of us waiting for her

so that we could fuck. "You two are so sexy," she said softly, and I thrust my cock slowly into Paige, filling her completely while her fingers rubbed her clit frantically.

Then I stopped, looking at Sierra expectantly. I was shocked that Paige spoke. "Please, Sierra, I'm so close."

A look of pure determination took over Sierra's face. "I've never watched anyone have sex before," she said tentatively, as I pulled out, then thrust deep. Paige's back arched, her entire body beginning to squirm with desperate need.

"You're so pretty," Sierra said softly. "Watching that huge cock sink into your… um." I stopped, and Paige cried out wordlessly.

"You're torturing her," I said quietly. "Obey your Master, Sierra. Keep talking."

She nodded. "Your cunt looks like it needs him. Like it needs to be fucked hard."

I picked up my pace, plunging deep and steady while Paige's fingers caressed her hot little button.

"Watching him fill you is hypnotic. I can't stop staring. He's so huge, and it looks like he wouldn't fit, but there it is, actually happening."

I noticed that Sierra's fingers had gently brushed her own clit a few times.

"I want to hear Paige come, Master. I want to hear her little noises when she comes for you. I want you to feel amazing, and come deep inside her."

Paige was right on the edge, moaning, "Don't stop, please, harder."

"Yes, harder, Master," Sierra said quickly, her voice getting a little higher as she babbled without thinking. "I want you to take her hard and fast, make her come. Make her feel it so deep, Master. Oh fuck, Master, I wish you were fucking me. Look at those gorgeous tits, her nipples look like they're on fire and need to be sucked. Suck her when she comes, Master. Drive her crazy."

Sierra's hand was almost a blur, fluttering lightly but quickly against her clit. I reached out to pinch Paige's nipples lightly just the way she likes.

Paige threw her head back in a scream, coming hard, her whole body writhing in ecstasy.

"Yes, Master," Sierra begged, "Fuck her harder as she comes. She's so fucking sexy for you Master, I bet she wants you to come inside her. Would that make you feel amazing? Fucking a hot girl while I watch, all tied up for you? I can't stand how intense it is watching you two. I..." Sierra cut herself off with a squeal, her head rolling back as she came, her fingers pressed firmly into her clit while I watched her. She came so beautifully, her body spasming gently then twitching slightly before relaxing completely, her huge eyes a bit glazed.

Paige sat up while I pulled out of her. "Thank you, Master," she said, giving me a kiss on the cheek before disappearing out the door. Sierra looked around, surprised.

Settling between her legs, I plunged into her luscious wetness. "My good girl," I said gently. "That was a challenge, to help you break through two walls at once. You were wonderful."

Her moan filled the room as I filled her snug pussy, and her fingers began brushing her clit again.

Bending down to kiss her, I murmured, "One day I will teach you orgasm control, and you will hover on the edge for as long as I tell you, no matter what I'm doing with you at the time. But today, I want to feel you come for me, Sierra. Let your gorgeous twat please your Master's cock."

"Yes, thank you, Master," she whispered.

Although she was tied up completely, her hips were still writhing, trying to buck up against me.

"Do you like being my little sex pet?" I asked suddenly, gripping her waist as I pounded into her harder, deeper.

"I've never been so happy in my entire life, Master," she said, looking directly into my eyes with honesty I wasn't expecting. "Do… do you want me to rub my clit faster and come for you now?"

"Yes."

Her shoulders began to shake as her mouth fell open, gasping as she brought herself to the edge. I've never been more proud of a submissive, and realized far too late that I was becoming lost in her.

*** SIERRA'S WISH COMES TRUE ***

The awkward humiliation had given way to pure pleasure, as I had the ultimate satisfaction of being fucked with a huge, perfect cock while touching my clit exactly how I needed it.

This was wild, depraved, crazy and I loved it. Watching the two of them have sex right in front of me had been the most sensual thing I'd ever seen in my life, but now Master was taking me hard and deep, my body his, chained, captive for his desires.

I felt the waves of energy gathering and hoped that he could feel my body begin to quiver. He must have, as he gripped me tighter, plunging hard and fast, taking me completely, owning me. He truly desired me, using me as his toy, and it was everything I'd ever dreamed of.

"Oh, Master…" I wailed, "I love the way… oh…" Orange and red fire licked through every nerve as I screamed, coming so hard I thought I might shatter from the intensity.

My body was humming, and I couldn't focus. I didn't realize at first that my leg restraints were gone, and my hands were being uncuffed while he thrust slowly inside me. Scooping me up against him, he held me practically up in his lap while ramming me deeper. I wrapped my arms around his shoulders, holding on while I bounced against him.

"Is this too hard?" he asked, watching my eyes.

I shook my head. "My body is yours. Make me ache for you, Master."

The light in his eyes changed, as that savage lust overtook him. Kissing me roughly, he pounded me as if to break me. "Yes, yes please, Master," I whimpered, "Harder."

His fingers dug into my shoulders as he pulled me down onto him against and again, his hips driving up as he shook. I could feel him begin to twitch inside me, and tried to tighten inside, clamping him tighter. The force of his release surprised me, and the primal growl against my lips as he came might have been even more satisfying to me than to him.

"Yes, Master," I breathed. "Fill your little pet."

His eyes were wild as he nodded slightly, warm bursts of cum flooding my pussy over and over as he held me. His kisses became more gentle, his hands stroking my back gently, as he pulled out, lying us down together.

He brushed my limp hair from my eyes, staring down at me with what may have been wonder. "Mine." I nodded. "My pet." I nodded again.

He pulled me against his chest suddenly, and I breathed in his warm, clean scent. His tanned, muscular physique made me feel so tiny and fragile next to him. I felt perfectly cared for, an unusual sensation.

Fingers snaked into the back of my hair, pulling my face to his. Those deep eyes were wild, savage. "Tell me how you feel, little one."

"Free, Master."

"Explain."

"I just did things I never would have imagined I could do."

"Why did you do them?"

"To please you. And myself. And to let poor Paige come," I laughed. "I needed to impress you, Master."

"But these were things that you did willingly, to get over your mental blocks?"

"Yes."

His lips crushed to mine for an instant. "I'm so proud of you, baby girl."

"Thank you, Master."

His lips moved to my ear as he breathed, "Every time you call me that my heart skips a beat." The way his arms were locked around me was so possessive that I felt strangely electrified.

He saw me glancing at his arms and smiled. "Mine. I don't care if it's not part of the program, you're sleeping with me tonight."

"Yes…" I said while licking my lips at him, "Master."

***

***

Training Sierra
(BDSM Training School Book #2)

*** JEREMY'S LESSONS ***

The BDSM Academy program was structured differently by every dominant. We each tried to provide a completely immersive environment for our submissives, but beyond that, the details varied greatly.

We each tried to deduce what we thought the submissive required, what we thought they needed to learn, and what we felt they needed to experience during their month of voluntary captivity with us.

Treating each individual as a completely submissive pet was a lot for some people to take. Although we told them in the beginning that they would be in the headspace twenty-four seven, most of the dominants could tell if a submissive was near the breaking point, and we would take them out of the headspace for the day.

Sometimes we might go shopping, to dinner or a movie, and just try to chat with them in a natural way about whatever they were having problems with.

Most of the time, it was simply fear. Fear of the unknown, fear of completely letting themselves go. In one case, I had a girl who began to fear that she was becoming addicted to sex and that there was something terribly wrong with her. Once I managed to get her to say that out loud, I made sure that we had no sexual contact for a few days, and then she was fine.

The thirty-day submissive program did not always include sex. Sometimes I would be compatible with a submissive, sometimes I wasn't. Sometimes I truly wanted them, but could feel that there was no spark between us, and they were not interested in me.

There were plenty of sensual services that they could perform for their Master that had no sexual element. A man does love a wonderful, intense foot or shoulder rub from time to time. Submissives can always learn to be intriguing and titillating without having to put out.

But with my darling little Sierra, we just seemed to fall for each other immediately and completely.

Since she had declared at the very beginning that she was dying to be a man's submissive sexual toy, and she obviously had a positive reaction with me, we have been nearly inseparable ever since. However, I had been very strict with her training, to make sure that she gets everything out of the program that she originally signed up for.

She has been kneeling for two hours a day while reading to condition her body. Stretching, toning, and practicing. I have tied her into incredibly intricate, restrictive bondage for hours at a time, and she has not once complained.

She has been studying every book I had given her, and when I quiz her every afternoon, she has obviously been working hard. She can get up from a kneeling position as graceful as a geisha, and was learning to anticipate my every move.

Sierra was an absolute delight, and I was finding it a fascinating creative challenge to try to think of interesting new things to do to her, and with her.

She had been with me for almost two weeks when I called for her in the afternoon. I knew that it was time to do something a tiny bit more aggressive to see how she would take it.

Sierra tapped at the door, then entered quietly, kneeling beside my bed. I could tell that she was already excited by the way her perky little nipples were at attention. I just adored that she hadn't worn clothing since she arrived, living completely naked except for her slim leather collar.

Since I called her into my bedroom instead of the office, she was probably expecting sex. But I needed to keep my gorgeous little darling on her toes.

"Up," I said, and she stood immediately, standing in front of me.

It was so difficult not to kiss her, but I had to maintain a bit of distance for at least a few minutes.

"My sweet little pet, it's time for you to be a good girl and impress your Master." She nodded eagerly.

"On your survey forms, you said that you had no experience with anal sex, but were interested in trying it." She immediately looked a bit nervous.

"Don't worry, my darling. I'm not going to be fucking you in the ass today."

She almost giggled, but maintained her composure.

"But I will be inserting a tiny butt plug so that you can begin to get used to the feeling."

Her mouth fell open in shock, but she closed it quickly, nodding slightly. "Yes, Master."

I sat on the bed, pulling out the small plug and a bottle of lube. "Over my knee."

She obeyed immediately, and I could see that she was trying to slow her breathing to relax her body.

I rubbed her back for a moment. I loved having her in this position for spankings, her body draped so gracefully over my legs. "Good girl. Don't worry, I'll be very gentle."

"Thank you, Master."

Rubbing a bit of lubricant on my fingers, I circled her

tiny opening slowly, watching how her shoulder blades twitched tightly every time I pressed against it. It took a few moments for her to really relax. She knew that I would be gentle, but it often takes a few minutes before our bodies catch up with our minds.

Pressing into her tightest tunnel just a bit, I stroked her back with my other hand. "Baby, I want you to think about the last time we fucked."

She nodded, grinning at me over her shoulder. It had been that morning, and I had taken her by surprise in the shower, pounding her up against the wall while her squeals echoed against the tiles.

"Remember how full you felt when I slid my cock inside you?"

"Yes, Master," she whispered.

Working my finger deeper, I asked, "You love it when your Master plays with your body, don't you?"

"Yes, Master."

"You love it when I take you, own you, possess you completely?"

She looked back at me with such absolute devotion in her eyes it was overwhelming. "Yes, Master." I tried not to allow my cock to jump up at her, but having her look at me that way shot spikes of adrenaline through me. This sweet little girl made me feel more masculine that I'd ever felt in my life.

Pressing deeper, I worked my entire finger into her tight asshole, taking slow, gentle strokes.

"Just think, sweetheart, someday when I take your luscious little ass, I will have taken you every way I can. Won't that be nice? Won't that be lovely to know that I own you completely?"

She released a sigh, nodding as her hips began to squirm in my lap. I didn't have to look down to know that she was getting wet.

Pulling my finger out gently, I coated the plug with lube, then held it out to show it to her. "See how tiny this is?" She nodded, unsure.

Spreading her legs a little, I circled her rosebud with just the tip of the plug. "That's my good girl. Just relax and open for your Master," I murmured.

She seemed to freeze up a little, but I pressed very gently, almost letting gravity do the work.

"That's it, baby," I said gently as I pushed it a bit deeper. "Just let your Master own your body completely."

She released a long, low sigh, and eventually the widest part of the plug slid gently into her, locking into position.

"That's my good girl," I murmured, quickly wiping my hands on a wet towel to remove the stickiness of the lube, then lying her gently on her back.

She gave a little gasp as her ass touched the bed, and the plug must have given her a tiny bit of pressure inside.

I should have had her remove my clothing, but after staring at her hot, peachy ass so long, I didn't want to waste the time. In seconds I was naked, on top of her, feeling her slim thighs spreading wide for me as I slid my hand between them.

Her nipples were so tight they almost looked like they hurt, as I wrapped my lips around one, sucking gently. As my fingers glided along her mound, her wet heat drew me in as I opened her slowly, sliding a finger inside.

"Do you like how that feels, with the pressure of your cute little butt plug, my pet?"

"Yes, Master," she breathed, wriggling slightly beneath me.

Moving to her other breast, I took her nipple between my teeth, scraping along the skin carefully while she moaned. Slipping a second finger inside, her silky wetness called to me. I was becoming spoiled, free to enjoy this treasure of a girl far too often, but I couldn't stop myself.

*** SIERRA, SO FULL ***

I still wasn't sure how I felt with this butt plug tightly wedged up my ass. The pressure was weird. It was sexy being in Master's lap while he slid it in, yet I still wasn't quite sure what I thought about the feeling.

But I adored the feeling of being owned by him, of my body being his to play with, so I tried hard to think of it as sexy. A measure of control, like my collar.

"My sweet little pet is wet for me," he growled softly, running his fingertips through my swollen pussy lips, swirling gently around my clit.

"I'm always wet for you, Master," I breathed, wrapping my arms around his shoulders. I could feel my hips starting to rock, opening as his fingers worked inside me.

He kissed me slowly, deeply, his hot tongue entering my mouth and stifling my constant moaning. As his fingers eased so softly into me, he rubbed against my throbbing clit with his thumb for just a moment, then pressed it gently with no movement.

I knew that he loved to tease me, but I was starting to lose control. He rounded his fingers slightly so that they were inside me, and the base of his thumb where it met the palm of his hand was pressing against my clit.

"Baby," he murmured, "I want to feel your hot little pussy dance against my hand. I want to kiss you while you come for me, humping my fingers."

I couldn't believe the strange, awkward things he had me do, but I knew that he was working hard to break down all of my mental walls.

"Yes, Master, I'll try," I whispered. Digging my heels into the bed slightly, I lifted my hips, pressing against him carefully.

"That's it, baby. Rub your luscious little pussy for me."

I was starting to feel almost feverish, surrounded by his

heat. I moaned, doing exactly what he wanted. I shamelessly began humping against his hand, working my wet, open twat against his thick fingers.

"Good girl," he whispered, kissing me with that desperate fire I loved.

I needed so badly to be fucked, but when he began wiggling his fingers slightly, curling them harder to press against my g-spot, I lost it. My hips began bucking against him faster, using him as a sex toy as he looked down at my trembling body.

Somehow this strange movement throughout my hips was making me feel even more open, and I was suddenly falling over the edge. I squealed as my energy peaked, coming desperately against his hand.

"My sweet little pet," he murmured when I slowed down. "Are you ready to do that again with your Master's cock?" I nodded eagerly.

He sat up, leaning against the headboard while I scooted into his lap. I loved it when he took me this way, and was already twitching in anticipation. Then I thought again about having his huge shaft in me while the plug was also filling me.

"Don't worry, my sweet pet, I know the plug is new for you. We'll go slowly."

I kissed his neck, working up to his ear lobe, nuzzling into him as I settled in his lap. I was rubbing my wet pussy lips up and down the length of his stiff cock without even thinking.

Suddenly he grabbed the back of my hair. "My sweet pet, you were touching your Master without permission."

"I… I'm sorry Master. I thought that's what you wanted."

"It is what I want, but I should punish you so that you don't forget these things again."

"Whatever pleases you, Master," I moaned, rubbing

harder against him, maneuvering us both so that his broad crown was pressing directly against my pussy lips.

Reaching down, I stroked his shaft, loving the heat that always filled it when he was hard for me.

He gripped my ass tightly, helping me to lower down onto his thickness slowly. The pressure was incredible. It was almost too much to take. The silicone plug deep in my ass was making me incredibly sensitive and pressing against my wet tunnel as he entered it.

"Master, you're stretching me so tight," I moaned, bearing down to take more of him in. He groaned, and I was thrilled once again that I could excite this sexy man as much as I seemed to.

"My sweet pet, you're even tighter with this plug in." He gripped my ass hard, lowering me just a little more.

I could feel my pussy dripping, so aroused that my body was almost out of control. His thickness was stretching my inner walls, feeling like it was rubbing against the plug. The feeling of my wonderful Master sliding so deeply into me was overwhelming me with sensation.

"Is this too much, baby?" he asked, searching my eyes anxiously.

"No, Master. This is wonderful."

He was almost completely inside me, a very tight fit, but I was so wet and squirming that he was able to push deeper. He bounced me slowly up and down, lifting me and lowering me until his long shaft slid completely inside, touching the very end of my passage.

"Oh," I moaned, my hips squirming even more. "Master, I love it when you're all the way inside me."

"Me too, my pet," he murmured, watching his thick shaft as it disappeared and reappeared through my wet pussy lips.

He spread my ass wider, tapping the butt plug gently with his finger, just enough to send the vibrations straight through me. I moaned again, moving against him in a deep, slow rhythm.

"My sweet baby, I think it's time for your punishment now."

I nodded, gasping, leaning forward so that he could easily reach my ass. He spanked me hard, several times on both sides, his rough hands feeling so perfect against my skin. I nuzzled into his neck, whining and squirming with every smack, as he increased the intensity.

"I love it when you are a bad girl for me," he growled, looking up at me as he gripped me hard with both hands. "I love spanking this gorgeous ass."

Undulating up and down, working him so deep inside me, I murmured into his ear, "Are you proud of your little girl for taking your huge cock in my tight, wet cunt, even with the toy inside me?"

He spanked me again, several times, then gripped me so hard his fingers were digging into my skin. "Such language from such a pretty girl."

"I can't help it," I whined. "You make me feel deliciously dirty, Master."

He thrust inside me, higher, deeper, then begin tapping the end of the plug again. Feeling this full was so intense that I didn't know if I could last much longer. The heat was rising inside me, and everything was beginning to hum.

"May I come for you, Master?"

"Only if you lean back so that I can watch you stroking your clit for me."

I was trying very hard not to be awkward about touching myself for him anymore, so I licked my fingers seductively, skimming them down my body until I latched on my clit. I leaned back so that he could watch my fingers rubbing into my little button slow and deep while his thickness filled me completely.

"Good girl," he moaned. "Open that sweet pussy wider

to take me deep."

I nodded, leaning back and spreading my legs even more, humping against him wildly. He took hold of the end of the butt plug, twisting it slightly, pulling out it just a pinch then pressing it deeper.

"Oh fuck," I gasped. "Yes, Master, fuck my pussy and my ass at the same time."

"My dirty little girl," he growled, his voice thick with desire. "Is my pet going to come all over my cock now?"

"May I, Master?"

"Yes, baby," he said, pounding me deeper while grinding the plug inside me in a matching pace. "Your Master needs to feel your soft little twat squirm for him."

"Oh," I whispered, suddenly quiet as a massive orgasm snuck up on me, crashing through my nerves, washing over me like a tidal wave.

"Oh, fuck, I can feel you, baby," he growled, gripping my ass harder. "I love the way you squeeze me when you come."

I gasped, then we were kissing, so hot and deep it was as if we were trying to swallow each other whole. His cock suddenly twitched deep within, coming hard as he spurted intensely inside my pussy walls, filling me even more than I thought possible.

"Yes," I whispered, our breath and tongues mingling as we writhed together.

After we rested, and he took the plug out for me, I realized that I really would be taking his cock there someday, and my curiosity made me dream about it all night long.

*** JEREMY CHECKS IN ***

I usually had a chat with submissives around the two-week mark to check in, and realized that it has already been that long with Sierra.

Tapping on her door first thing in the morning, she sounded surprised. "Come in?"

"Hey there, sweetie."

She was naked, on the floor in a yoga stretch. Instantly jumping up, she knelt at my feet. "Good morning, Master."

I pet her hair for a moment, then sat on her bed, tapping the spot beside me. "Sierra, it's time for us to check in with how you're doing." Her eyes instantly flashed with a tinge of fear, and I felt it painful to realize she always defaulted to not feeling good enough. She sat beside me nervously, with her hands clasped in her lap.

"Baby, please don't be nervous. I think everything is wonderful. But it's been two weeks, and it's always good to step back and see how things are going. So, we can drop the formalities for now, and just be open. How are you doing? How do you feel about your time here so far?"

Her eyes lit up. "I love it here. I've never felt like I was in the right place. I've always been sort of… out of sync with the world, I guess. But here I know what's going on. I feel like I know my place. And I'm learning so much. Not just about protocol and how to behave as a submissive, but I've learned so much about myself."

I reached out to touch her, but realized at the last second that being sexual at all right now would be wrong, so I just patted her knee for a moment. "I'm so glad. What have you learned?"

"I function much better with a schedule," she said brightly. "I've never slept very well, but now that I'm on a schedule most of the time, and I read before bed, I've been sleeping brilliantly. And I don't get indigestion any more, because I eat three meals a day instead of one big one. Oh – and I'm much more flexible and calm because I spend an hour stretching with soft music on. It's sort of like meditation."

She had never spoken so much about herself. It was delightful.

"What else?"

Sierra looked at the floor for a moment, thinking. "I've always wanted to be a man's sexual toy, and now that I know what that truly feels like, I know that it wasn't just fantasy, it's reality." She shot me a little grin. "Some fantasies are better left in the back of your mind. But this one is certainly real. And…"

She blushed beautifully, while I gave her knee a little shake. "You can tell me. Go on."

Taking a deep breath, she blurted, "I never saw myself as a very sexual girl before. I didn't realize what a big part of my life it could be, or should be. But with you, all the time, and always so different… I've learned so much about my body, and what I want and need. I… I feel, um." She looked up at me with those big soft eyes. "I've never felt sexy before. Not really, to the core. It's… wow."

It was incredibly hard not to wrap my arms around her at that moment. "Sierra, you are a sexual goddess. A vision. I've never seen a woman light up from within the way you do. I've never had a woman drive me as crazy as you do. One of the things I needed to ask you today is if we've been having too much sex. Is it too much for you?"

She shook her head emphatically. "No. Not at all."

"But you know that you can say, 'no thank you, not right now' at any time, right?"

Sierra nodded. "Yes. I know. I like to fall completely into our… I don't want to call it a game, but you know what I mean. Our S&M headspace. But I always know in the back of my mind that I could call red, or say no."

She looked up at me with a grin. "But I don't think I'd ever need to. You read me so well that if I was ever hesitant about something, you'd see it in my eyes, or see the tension in me somehow. I feel like I wouldn't need to say it – you'd already know."

My hand was suddenly against the center of her back, stroking her petal-soft skin gently. "I do try to read you. The only thing you were truly hesitant about so far was the butt plug, and I watched your shoulders so carefully. You were nervous, but you really did want to try it. Right?"

She nodded. "Yes."

"So you feel safe with me? I've never crossed any lines, or made you feel uncomfortable?"

Her eyes grew wide. "No. Never. Not even close."

"And you want to continue for the next two weeks, progressing pretty much as we have been?"

She nodded eagerly. "Yes. Please."

"Is there anything you need that you're not getting? Anything you wish to learn that we haven't tried yet?"

Concentrating for a moment, her lips pressed together while she thought. "I don't know."

"Besides anal sex, is there anything you haven't tried?" The little flush that crept across her cheeks was a sign. "You don't have to tell me, of course. But if there is anything you'd like to explore, you're in a safe place for experimentation."

She nodded. "Okay. Well, I've never been with a woman, and I've always been curious. But that's not something you could help with."

I laughed suddenly, surprising her. "Sweetie, I have Chloe and Paige available at any time, or I could give you a folder full of submissives I could call and have them here tomorrow."

I noticed that her hands began to flutter, and reached out to hold them still. "Shh, it's okay. You can think about it.

There's no need to rush. Let it roll around in your mind for a while."

"Okay. Thank you."

"Anything else you might like to try?"

"I don't know."

"Have you ever played in public before?"

Her pretty little lips fell open. "No," she whispered.

I reached up to drag my thumb lightly across her breast. "From the way your nipples just twitched and your pupils grew wide, the thought of being fucked with an audience turns you on."

She stared at me, then nodded slightly.

"There is a private dungeon party Friday night. There are usually around thirty to forty people in attendance. Not a cheering crowd of thousands, but likely enough to get you humming."

Sierra's grin was enchanting. Then she cocked her head. "What day is it today?"

I laughed. "It's Tuesday."

She nodded.

"You think about that as well, and I'll ask you again soon."

"Okay. Thank you."

"Is there anything you've wanted to ask me, or tell me, or get off your chest?"

She shook her head. "I don't think so."

I tipped her head up with a finger under her chin, watching her eyes. "Do you want to feel my cock deep in your hot little ass?"

Her pupils dilated, and the smile was genuine. "Yes, Master."

I patted her knee again. "Good. I'll put that on the list." I stood up to leave. "Breakfast, and I'll call for you later."

"Wait." I turned back to her. "Um, are you, you know… getting everything you need from me?"

My arms were around her in a flash, pulling her against me roughly. "Baby, you are a dream. I've never had a submissive as bright, intuitive, sexy, and charming as you. You're everything I've ever wanted and more."

Her arms wrapped around my shoulders, holding tight. She looked like she wanted to speak, but couldn't bring herself to say it.

"Whatever it is, you can tell me. Or ask. Really."

"Not yet."

"Okay." I held her tightly, cuddling her for a few minutes before releasing her. Kissing the top of her head, I murmured, "See you soon, baby."

It was difficult to leave without throwing her across her little bed and taking her right there, but our official meetings needed to be reserved for open discussion only.

I knew what she wanted to ask. She wants to stay with me. I can feel it, or at least I think I can. And as much as I desperately wanted to keep her forever, I felt like it was too soon to make that call. After I saw how she played in public, and shook a few more of her fears out, I could decide then.

*** SIERRA TIED UP ***

I was so excited when he called me into his bedroom again so soon. His schedule seemed a bit erratic, with only mealtimes remaining steady. It was wonderful that he worked from home so that he was able to spend so much time with me, and I truly appreciated him teaching me as much as he did.

At this point, I didn't know whether I could even imagine living out in the regular world again. Everything in this huge mansion made sense to me. The people had their places, and were always willing to help each other. Master ran the house, and there were no unanswered questions. There was comfort here. Peace.

Although, as I tapped on his door and walked to his feet, quiet as a whisper, I hoped there would be excitement soon.

Kneeling quickly, my wrists held behind my back, I looked to the floor while trying to appear calm.

"How long are you able to kneel without pain now, little one?"

"At least two hours, Sir. Then I quickly stretch and begin again, as you instructed."

He patted the top of my head, then went back to the bed where he was fussing around with some bondage gear. I could feel everything within me stir with excitement. Just because he was tying me up didn't necessarily mean we'd be having sex soon, but the odds were pretty good.

A few times he had trussed me up and left me for a long time. I know that he's teaching me patience, and self-discipline. But also self-awareness. When one is in bondage, you must constantly be scanning your body to make sure everything is truly okay. It's one thing for something to pinch for a few minutes, but if it's going to be for a long time, or if weight is going to put on the area, a submissive must speak up before they are injured.

I heard of a girl who was in a rope suspension and didn't rotate her hands in the ties every few minutes. She had nerve damage in her left arm, and her hand felt like it was drunk for a week. She was extremely lucky – for some it takes months for the sensation to come back.

I was meticulous with checking my position, wiggling and rotating what I could, and I even studied some anatomy books so I knew where the most easily damaged nerves were.

It was wonderful impressing Master with my new knowledge, but now I knew that he would be finding even more adventurous ways to tie me up.

"Up."

I stood gracefully, smoothly, as I had practiced. He nodded toward the bed, and I climbed up, kneeling. He quickly tied a rope chest harness, and I saw that some of the chains and bars were hanging from the hard points on the ceiling.

Within moments, my chest was suspended from above, but my hands were also gripping a bar. It was remarkably comfortable with approximately seventy percent of my weight being held from my core, and the rest from my arms.

I was hung so that my knees were only three inches off the bed, then Master used a remote control, and I lifted into the air another inch.

As much as I had been practicing perfect control, I couldn't help giggling. It seemed to be alright, as he grinned and chuckled back at me.

"Hang tight, gorgeous," he said, then he came up on the bed to bend my knees snugly, wrapping them with leather strips until my ankles were just under my bum.

He lowered me again so that my knees touched the bed, relieving the weight. "Does anything pinch or place pressure in a bad area?" he asked, his eyes quickly skimming me as he poked and prodded.

"Not at all, Master. This is surprisingly comfortable, thank you."

Gripping the back of my head, he suddenly pulled me against him in a ferocious kiss. He always seemed a little more dominant when I was immobilized, which thrilled me to the core.

I loved the way he controlled me. It was illogical, and I didn't care. Giving myself to Master completely, allowing him to own me, had freed my mind in a way I could never have imagined. When he was more aggressive, I felt even more desired.

He stared at me for a while, checking his ties to make sure that I was totally safe, then he stared at me a little differently. As if he were trying to decide what to do with me next.

He must have made a decision, as he began unbuttoning his shirt, slowly. As I watched him pull it off, I couldn't believe how handsome he was. Those wide, strong shoulders always made me feel so protected, even when he was using his thick arms to spank me.

His belt hit the floor, and he removed his pants, kicking them aside. Joining me on the bed, he kissed me again with that fire that always seemed to flow between us.

Then I was rising into the air until our lips parted. I loved the way he was often so playful, laughing with me as the slight mechanical hum pulled me upward.

He laid down with his head on a pillow, then lowered me carefully until my legs spread on either side of his face. I descended very slowly until he could comfortably lick me with no pressure on his face. It was absolutely fascinating, as he reached up to my open, excited pussy and spread me open.

He ran his thumbs along my outer lips, then nuzzled my mound, kissing and sucking and licking everywhere. He was teasing me with his tongue, taking his time. Somehow my thighs spread a little wider as I tried to remain still for him, yet my hips were swirling slightly.

"Be still, sweet baby," he murmured softly, but with that authority in his deep voice that could not be ignored.

"I'm trying, Master."

I tried to relax my shoulders, quiet my breathing, and let my body be still for him. But I felt my swollen pussy begin to gush as he licked and sucked. He slipped a finger inside me, circling my inner lips then gliding in.

It was so perfectly erotic being so open for him. I was completely defenseless, helpless, and he was almost torturing me with pleasure. He pressed his tongue against my throbbing clit, licking firmly, then so gently it was almost a tease.

Trying not to buck my hips against him was almost impossible, but I tried my very best. My hands were clenched on the bar as I hung in the air, quivering with too much desire flooding through me.

Master slid a second finger inside me, circling my swollen button then lashing his tongue across it. "Good girl," he said softly. "Open yourself to me completely."

I absolutely adored it when he gave me an order when I was so close to the edge. Every stroke of his long, thick fingers inside me brought me closer to the peak, and the way he was licking me, so wet and deep, my entire body was beginning to twitch.

"Master, may I come for you?"

"Not yet, baby."

He began rubbing his tongue firmly over my swollen button, fucking me harder with his fingers. It felt like my entire body was clenching around his hand and pressing against his tongue. I could feel it in my shoulder blades, down my spine. It almost felt like I was drowning in pleasure.

"Please Master, please let me come for you."

"Not yet, baby."

Desperately trying to calm my breathing, I felt every muscle pulling inward, trying to stop the force of my orgasm from hitting me completely. I felt like if I so much as blinked too hard I would lose all control.

Looking down into his gorgeous deep eyes, he could see that I was twitching as if my entire body was one exposed nerve that was feeling too much.

He gave me a wink, then murmured, "Come now."

A third finger joined the rest, fucking me hard and deep as his tongue slid lightly over my most delicate flesh. I screamed, falling over the edge until my nerves and pulse and emotions were all tumbling through me in one frazzled wave of absolute bliss.

The intensity was too much to take, but it felt so beautiful, rolling through me in waves as I seemed to come for a very long time.

As everything finally ebbed, I caught my breath, whispering, "Thank you, Master."

He slid out from under me, lowering me so that my weight was now on my knees on the bed. He knelt in front of me, wrapping his arms around me and just holding me while I quivered.

"I love it when you let me own you completely," he said softly, stroking my hair.

I wasn't sure whether I was going to burst into tears, a fit of laughter, or zone out into a zombie state. His hands stroked my back over the rope harness, and then he pulled back to look into my eyes.

"Have you had enough?"

"No, Master. I'm fine."

"Do you want more like this, or should I untie you?"

I realized that there was probably something else he would like to try while I was all tied up like this, then I suddenly could not control my giggling.

"I have a feeling that Master might like to hang me from the ceiling for just a little bit longer," I laughed.

Cupping my cheek in his large hand, he studied my eyes. "Only if you can handle being suspended again."

"I'm fine, really. Everything feels good. Thank you for letting me take this break to catch my breath after that amazing orgasm, Master."

He kissed my nose, then said, "Hold on tight." Raising me slowly up in the air again, he laid under me, lining up our bodies before lowering me again.

*** MASTER'S SEXY TOY ***

I always adored how my sweet little girl was so docile and obedient, but when she allowed me to tie her up completely, I was overwhelmed by the feeling of ownership. She was completely mine.

I have had submissives before, but never with as much light and life as this special girl. The gift of her body was incredible, but she had given her entire self to me. Our bond was growing stronger every day.

Watching her giggle with delight as I raised her up made me laugh along with her. Moving underneath her quickly, I lined us up so that when I lowered her again, she was straddling my hips.

I was nearly always hard when she was around, but after tasting her for so long, feeling her quiver on my tongue, my cock was absolutely straining to touch her. It stood up, veins bulging, throbbing with need.

She instinctively leaned forward, trying to angle her pussy so that I could enter her. I didn't know which of us I was teasing more when I lined us up, pressing my head between her wet inner lips, not quite entering her. I could feel her twitching, so eager to take me in. But she was trying so hard to appear calm for me. I admired how she always tried her absolute best, even when she was being driven crazy.

Her torso seemed to lengthen, her arms straining, as her body tried to lower itself. Setting the remote to more precise increments, I lowered her three millimeters. Feeling my head sink into her softness was too tempting for me to wait any longer, and I lowered her more, slowly. She writhed above me, so eager to take me in.

"Does my little pet want more?"

"Please, Master. You know I do."

Lowering her gradually, her hips squirmed until I was

deep in her tender pussy. She couldn't stop squirming, and her swinging motion was overpowering. Her desperation was causing my pulse to race, my blood hammering through my veins.

From the moment I met Sierra, I felt more dominant around her than anyone ever before. But the way her entire body was begging desperately for me, so needy and open... I felt my aggression begin to lose control.

Dropping her another half inch so that a bit of her weight was on my hips, she moaned, using her arms to lift her body up and down. She was fucking herself. It was the most erotic, gorgeous thing I'd ever seen. Her cheeks and throat were flushed, eyes closed, breathing in rapid pants as she exhaled, "Oh, oh..."

Bringing my thumb to her clit, she bucked even more. Watching her little biceps flexing as she hoisted herself up and down on my shaft was amazing. Any self consciousness was completely dissolved as she brazenly fucked me, gasping and moaning.

Pressing into her hot, swollen clit harder, I angled my hips, thrusting into her deeper.

"Oh fuck, yes," she moaned.

I was unable to blink for fear of missing one moment of this intoxicating vision. She was straining, pulsing, savagely shoving her body onto mine as her wet heat enveloped my cock while she squeezed me hard. My balls began to tighten and I knew I couldn't last much longer.

"Come for me, pet," I growled, and her screams began at the first word. Her hot little body overloaded, impaling herself recklessly over and over while she wailed, lost in sensation.

Gripping her ass hard, I joined her, roaring as I thrust up into her luscious twat, coming harder than I ever had in my life.

We shook wildly together, then her eyes opened,

dazed. I lowered her completely, lying her on her side. Her breathing was still erratic as I unfastened the chest harness quickly, then her legs. She lay in a heap of rope and leather strips, finally looking up to me.

"Hi," she said weakly.

I pushed everything out of the way and slipped a pillow under her head. "Baby, are you okay?"

She nodded. "That was... Weird."

"Yes," I said, stroking her hair gently, but giving her some space. "You went a bit crazy, sweetheart. What happened?"

Staring at the ceiling for a moment, her eyes seemed to refocus. "I came so hard when you were licking me, then I wanted to feel you fuck me, then... my body needed you so badly it sort of overloaded, I guess." She looked up at me, embarrassed. "I'm sorry."

"No, sweetheart, that was the hottest fucking thing I've ever seen. It just worried me a little."

"I felt so free," she whispered, almost to herself. "I finally let go."

"I'm so proud of you," I said, stroking her back. "But you're going to bed early tonight to sleep off that adrenaline. Okay?"

She nodded, smiling dreamily. "Yes, Master."

*** SIERRA'S SPANKING ***

I tried to concentrate, but since we had our little chat, there was only one thing on my mind. I begged him so often that it felt like second nature, but I couldn't bring myself to beg for this. I needed him to keep me, but that had to be his decision. If I begged, he might consider taking me on as his full time submissive out of guilt or obligation. That wasn't right.

I would wait until he brought it up, but it was heavily on my mind. I felt closer to him every time we were together and the way I was able to totally let go last night was mind blowing.

The thought of playing in public terrified and delighted me. I knew it was a big deal to some people, and perfectly natural for others, but didn't know where I fell on the spectrum. I just knew that it was something he wanted, so I wanted to give it to him. And if I hadn't tried it yet, I didn't know if I liked it.

When he called for me the next morning, I was already aroused just from thinking about what he would do to me with an audience. As I knelt at his bare feet, I was certain he could tell what sort of state I was in.

"Up. Undress me."

Rising as gracefully as possible, I met his eyes. He was amused, light-hearted. I flashed him a grin, then began unbuttoning his shirt slowly, revealing his broad, tan chest. My hand looked so pale against his skin as I pulled the fabric off, tossing it over a chair.

Unfastening his belt, I started to throw it onto the chair, but he said, "I'll need that on the bed." I looked up at him, stunned, but he was still smiling.

Tossing the thick leather belt onto the bed, I tried to stop my hands from trembling as I unbuttoned his pants, pulling them down over his hips and down his strong legs.

He sat on the bed, crooking his finger and motioning for me to lie over his lap. I remembered the first time he spanked me, and although I was impossibly aroused, it was a little too much. But he used the pain to make me blurt out things I couldn't quite bring myself to say.

Now I enjoyed his spankings, especially since I knew what they usually led to. But having that thick belt lying within arm's reach was a bit unnerving.

I laid across the tops of his thighs in spanking position, and he began to caress my skin. He gave me a tiny playful smack on each cheek.

"I know that you're a shy little sparrow sometimes, my sweet pet," he said gently, running his fingers up and down my spine almost hypnotically. "But I need you to be absolutely honest so that I can help you grow."

"Yes, Master."

His hand snapped sharply against my right cheek. I exhaled slowly, breathing the pain out until it was only pure sensation.

"Sierra," he asked, turning my head gently so that our eyes met. "Do you want to lick a girl's pussy, and feel her come under your tongue?"

I nodded, not avoiding a spanking, but feeling that I could be absolutely honest with him, and myself now.

He grinned, looking so boyishly handsome that my heart melted all over again. "And you want to feel a woman take care of you?"

"Yes, Master."

He caressed my ass, knowing now that he didn't need to shock the truth out of me. "And would you prefer to be alone with her, or have me watch?"

"I…" I giggled at his surprised expression. "It never occurred to me that you wouldn't be there, Master."

"If you prefer to have that experience alone, I understand. Of course I would like to watch, but that's up to you."

I didn't mind either way, but could tell he would love to watch me. That thrilled me to the core. "I'd like to have you watching. I think that would excite me even more."

His hands skimmed over my skin, and I felt his arousal pressing against me from below. Wiggling just slightly, I tried to line him up between my legs.

He gave me the tiniest smack on my left cheek. "And have you thought about playing in public?"

The way he was studying my eyes so carefully was magical. "Yes. I would like to serve you in every way possible, Master. You may use me for anything and everything you like. Privately, publicly, I am yours."

He lowered his lips to my ear, murmuring, "You want a room full of people to hear your little squeals as I throw you against a wall and fuck you hard?"

My involuntary moan answered for me.

He grabbed the belt, but I somehow knew he wasn't going to hit me with it. Standing me up, he wrapped it around my wrists, roughly strapping them together in front of me.

"On your back on the bed," he commanded.

My nipples were throbbing, my pussy was getting wet, and my heart was already racing, just from knowing that Master could do absolutely anything he wanted to me. I never knew what was next, and it was such a thrill.

Lying on my back, I got comfortable, waiting excitedly.

*** MASTER TAKES CONTROL ***

Standing up, I stripped quickly, then climbed onto the bed, straddling her shoulders as I swiped the tip of my cock along her lips. Her arms were trapped at her sides, so I had complete control as I eased my thickness between her lips.

Her eyes lit up, absolutely delighted that she could bring me pleasure. I know that she's been working very hard to take my length completely, and as I gently pressed down her throat, I was extremely impressed.

Rocking gently, taking deep slow strokes into her warm mouth, I couldn't believe how lucky I was to have such a perfect, beautiful toy to play with every time I wanted.

I couldn't think about what would happen in just a few more weeks when our time was up, and had to focus on every day as if it were the last.

Her tongue fluttered around my sensitive head every time I pulled out, and her mouth sucked me deep with every stroke. The pressure was perfect, and I could have come in seconds, but I somehow managed to hold myself back, looking into her dazzling eyes as she served me.

As much as I adored the feeling of her soft, wet mouth, I was somehow even more aroused by the knowledge she was giving herself to me completely.

In my opinion, it took an exceedingly strong woman to give her power away, and being brave enough to let someone else control her.

But even though I was pinning her down, sinking my rock hard shaft between her lips, she was still controlling my pleasure. Her quick little tongue lapped up a bead of pre-cum dripping from my head when I pulled it from her lips. Then as I plunged deep, she licked the underside, her tongue darting along my most sensitive area.

Her muffled moans drove me crazy, and I glanced down to see that her hands were curled into fists as she concentrated, sucking me deeper, harder.

Her wide bright eyes stared up at me, as she brought her head forward, bobbing on my cock even though I was completely fucking her mouth. My shaft was throbbing against her lips, and she had me more aroused than any woman ever has before.

Reaching behind me, I slid my hands between her legs, giving her inner thigh a tiny slap so she would open for me. Her eyes smiled as I stroked her luscious softness. Digging my fingers deep inside her, she moaned against my cock, always focused on my pleasure, while reveling in her own.

Pumping my fingers faster into her sweet little cunt, the feeling of her body squirming beneath me was intensifying. Her tongue lapping along my skin was causing everything to tingle and pulse, and I felt myself beginning to lose my concentration.

Her sweet honey began to really flow against my hand, as I thumbed her clit gently. But I couldn't stop rocking my hips harder, thrusting deep, fucking the beautiful mouth of my sweet submissive toy.

"Does my baby girl want to swallow?" She nodded slightly, restrained but so eager to please me.

Her cheeks hollowed out as she sucked harder, thrusting her head up, pressing her lips firmly against my throbbing cock. My entire body rattled for a moment, shuddering hard as I came deep in her soft, sweet mouth. She was moaning just as loudly as I was, while she slurped and swallowed, never wasting a drop.

When I pulled my shaft from her lips, leaning back to thrust my fingers harder into her softness, she murmured, "You are delicious, Master."

Her wide-eyed obedience was almost too much to take, and a dominant is never supposed to appear flustered. But I was almost high from her magical energy.

I quickly rolled off of her, removing the belt around her

wrists, then lying beside her and giving her shoulders a little massage.

"Was I too heavy on your shoulders, baby?"

She smiled, not quite rolling her eyes. "No, I'm fine, thank you, Master."

I grabbed her roughly, rolling her on top of me, her tiny gasp caught in her throat.

"Wrists behind your back," I ordered, and she grasped them quickly, collapsing against my chest.

My arms gripped her tightly, as I kissed her neck, inhaling her fresh, sweet scent that always felt like some weird primal pheromones were washing over me.

Feeling the length of her body pressed against mine, she arched her back slightly to wriggle her breasts against my chest and her hips against my quickly thickening shaft. Her lips were close to my ear, and her whimpered moan, so breathy and desperate, did me in.

Spreading her legs completely with my knee, I gripped her round, firm ass, as my cock pressed against her clit, rubbing hard a few dozen times before sinking gently inside her.

She cried out, her knees falling to straddle my hips as my teeth grazed against the delicate skin of her neck. Her silky skin glided against mine as I drove deep. My fingers sunk into her behind as I pulled her down, her pussy welcoming me in.

Searing my lips to hers, she was practically panting as she kissed me, driving her hips into mine, fucking us both wildly. Her slippery little cunt was so soft, so snug, the way her body clamped down against me was too much pleasure for one man to take.

"Arms over your head."

She obeyed in a heartbeat, then I flipped her onto her back, my hips pushing forward as she moaned against my lips. Driving inch after thick inch of my cock into her pussy, her legs wrapped around my waist until we were pinned together.

She gripped my shoulders, I grabbed her waist, and we were suddenly fiercely fucking like animals. The way Sierra was moaning into my lips made me feel more dominant than any bondage, any punishment, any pleading I'd ever heard from a submissive.

She was so utterly, thoroughly mine that I felt my control slipping again, grinding into her hard and fast as her little cries of bliss filled my ears.

She was a drug I needed more of. A taste I always desired but could never quite satiate me. She made me feel greedy for her, even as my cock crushed deep into her wetness, harder than I've ever fucked her before.

"Master, may I come for you?" she gasped, her body almost convulsing already.

"Wait, my little pet."

I knew that it would take some more time to teach her total orgasm control, but at this moment I simply wanted her release to trigger my own, after I had enjoyed her a little longer.

I suddenly remembered that I should be working on her training, even right now.

"Tell me what you're feeling, baby. You know I love it when you talk dirty for me."

Even as I was ramming inside her, this made her blush slightly. It was extremely difficult for her to speak in moments like this, which is why I tried to encourage her to break down her barriers.

"You feel incredible, Master. You know I love the feeling of your cock inside me."

"Tell me how it feels, my sweet pet. Tell me everything."

*** SIERRA SPEAKS UP ***

I could take almost any punishment. I was learning to accept levels of pain and discomfort with patience and grace. But talking dirty, describing physical sensations, and trying to speak during sex was extraordinarily frustrating for me. I knew that Master just wanted to push my limits and help me, but I wish he would just let me enjoy the sex.

Remembering that being submissive was all about service, I tried to give my mind a little shake and get back into the correct headspace.

I was here to serve my Master. I was here to give him everything he wanted. And I was here to learn how to become his perfect toy. Taking a deep breath, I closed my eyes for a moment and prepared to feel embarrassed and awkward. Anything for him.

"The pressure of your huge cock inside me is overwhelming, Master. Sometimes when you fuck me hard, it's right up against the edge of pain, holding me tightly right in that weird sweet spot that drives me perfectly insane."

"Good girl. Keep going."

Oh God, he was fucking me so deeply, so possessively, that I was having serious trouble holding back my climax.

"I love it when you use my body, Master. I always love serving you, but when you take hold of me, owning me, filling me, I feel like my entire body turns into one giant nerve, processing too much input until I short-circuit."

"Creative. Keep going." He bit gently at my throat, making me gasp and moan.

"I love swallowing your cum. I love the look in your eyes just before you let go. When your cum fills my little pussy, I feel so satisfied. Complete. Like it's what my body has been needing for my entire life."

I took a breath, and he nodded at me again.

"Please Master, I need to come so badly. You've been

rubbing against my clit so perfectly, for so long that I can't… It's hard to hold back. Don't you want to feel my cunt all wet and squirming for you?"

He just looked at me, smiling and nodding.

"Don't you love the feeling when my little pussy grips you tightly? When you make me come so hard my entire body shakes for you?"

"Yes, baby, you know how much I love that."

I bit my lip, looking up at him, trying to look as positively desperate as I felt. "Master, please may I come?"

We moved together, my legs locking around him tightly as I pulled him deeper. I was pretty sure that I felt him beginning to swell even more inside me, and needed to feel him finally lose control.

"Fill me with your cum, Master," I whined. "The feeling of it when it gushes inside me… It's so perfect."

He gripped me hard, and I thought I could feel his control slipping as well.

"Tell me what you wouldn't tell me yet in your room."

His eyes were burning into mine as hard as his cock was driving into my pussy, the friction so intense my entire body was screaming, and I couldn't hold anything back any longer.

The words came out in a choked, desperate cry. "I want to stay with you, Master. I want you to own me forever. Being your pet is my entire life."

"Come now."

"Thank you, Master," I gasped, then I was screaming into his mouth as he kissed me, ramming me into the bed so hard I was practically bouncing as my pussy exploded around his cock. I absolutely convulsed as I came, squirming and accidentally scraping his shoulders with my fingernails as I gripped him desperately.

"Good girl," he growled, my pulsing pussy driving him over the edge as he rammed harder, filling me with his hot juices while I gasped and moaned. His groan, his racing heart, knowing that I pleased him – it was so unbelievably satisfying.

"Yes, oh yes," I cried, until we came to a panting, breathless stop.

I was nervous about what I had said, but I knew that he would already have known what I was thinking.

His arms wrapped around me gently as we curled up, just breathing together. I was too terrified to speak, waiting for him to say something.

"It's very early. Let's make sure we're right, baby. We'll know in two more weeks."

"Yes, Master." I shut my eyes tightly so that he couldn't see my tears of joy, but I knew he could feel me trembling.

"Shh, it's okay, baby," he whispered, kissing along the outer shell of my ear. His arms held me tighter, as he rocked me gently. Master always knew.

***

Teasing Sierra
(BDSM Training School Book #3)

*** MASTER GOES OUT FRIDAY NIGHT ***

I had been to countless dungeon parties, with a variety of lovely ladies on my leash. But I'd never been as proud as I was when I walked into the huge softly lit room leading Sierra on a silver chain. She looked so innocent and sweet, wearing only her little collar, a completely transparent black dress, and tiny flat shoes.

Watching the others admire my pet was an ego-boost, but even though I was playing the part of the social dominant, a member of the BDSM Academy, I was actually focused on her. She had never been to an event like this that permitted absolutely everything. Plus, she had been fairly isolated from the world for a few weeks. My concentration was on her comfort above all else, even though I desperately wanted to drag her to the play area and take her immediately.

My hand against the center of her back seemed to steady her, and she glanced up at me with a tiny smile. I raised my eyebrow, and she nodded. Walking into the room and over to a group of people I knew, Sierra glided behind me, quiet and smooth as a shadow.

Joining my old friends, I could feel her presence as she knelt at my feet, and my hand automatically fell to her hair, petting her gently. I don't think I could have stopped touching her even if I wanted to.

Even while I was laughing at Patrick's tales of a submissive who was too ticklish to tie down, I felt the top of Sierra's head pressing up into my hand. She wasn't trying to distract me, just feel her.

By the time Kate was finishing a story of her latest boy toy being so devoted that he was risking a sprained tongue, I realized I didn't have it in me to be polite any longer.

"Excuse me, folks," I said, "I need to test my little pet's reaction to the dungeon."

Although we had not discussed all signals, a single tap of my finger on her head caused Sierra to rise gracefully, standing behind me. I loved how she was always ready for anything. This kind of open-mindedness cannot be taught. It is ingrained, or not.

She excelled at everything I tested her with. She was ready to be a permanent submissive already, I was sure of it. But I did need to give her a little more time so that she could make an informed decision.

It was tricky being someone's dominant, and having total control. Ultimately, I was attempting to give her everything she wanted and needed, so she was the one controlling the situation, but I had to keep up the feeling that she was only doing my bidding.

I knew that she truly adored being dominated completely – her physical reactions were obvious. But I was still careful since she was nervous about new things. If she changed her mind at any moment, I was prepared to wrap her back up in her trench coat and take her home immediately.

But the feeling of owning her in public was a thrill I sincerely hoped that she'd be into. It was a silly decadence that thoroughly aroused me, and I'd never had a partner who was so gorgeous, so completely submissive that she drove me this wild.

*** SIERRA'S SPANKING AND MORE ***

While outwardly attempting to appear calm, like the perfect little submissive, my guts were fluttering with nerves. I'd never really played in public beyond a few spankings and floggings, and had no idea what Master had in store for me.

I knew that he enjoyed surprising me, and I wasn't certain if it was to keep me reactive and on my toes, or whether he enjoyed my little expressions of surprise. It was startling how much I seemed to amuse him. I felt like I was truly pleasing him. And I had to hope that if I proved myself worthy, he would keep me forever.

As I shadowed him to the dungeon play area at the back of the enormous room, I noticed that everyone seemed to nod to him in greeting. I knew that he was a well-known figure of this loosely constructed organization, but he seemed to be one of the leaders.

He led me to a spanking bench in the farthest corner. It was my favorite piece of equipment, and for a moment my excitement leaped into my throat at the thought of being fucked doggy-style while cuffed to the bench. Then I looked around at the forty to fifty people milling around throughout the space and became slightly nervous.

Master spun me, hooking his finger into the ring of my collar and tilting my face up to him. "My sweet pet," he grinned. "You're so gorgeous that you were distracting me while I was speaking with my friends."

"I'm sorry, Master."

He found the most ridiculous excuses to punish me, and it was sometimes difficult not to giggle. He pulled me against him for a swift, rough kiss, and I felt my knees suddenly become less dependable.

"I need to ask you before you get all adrenaline high, baby. And you need to know, I'm not judging you either way. I don't want you to try to please me. I want you to feel safe with me."

I nodded, not sure where he was going with this.

"If you want to have a little spanking and go home, that's fine. Or, if you truly want to, I could fuck you so hard you scream while a few of these nice people watch."

I hoped that he could see that my grin was genuine. "I'm a little nervous Master, but only because it's my first time in public. Yes – please take me. Use your toy any way you like."

The glint in his eyes made me feel extremely proud, as I could see it was the precise answer he was hoping for. But it was also how I truly felt. Doing something so incredibly intimate in front of strangers was so audaciously wrong. Completely filthy. So obviously, I couldn't wait.

"Up."

I followed his hand gesture and knelt on the step of the bench. As he took hold of the hem of my dress, I raised my arms. Not that the dress had been really covering me, and everyone had been checking me out since I entered the room, it had felt like I was dressed.

Now the slight breeze of the ceiling fan was skimming across my nipples and all the way down my spine.

Master laid me face down on the bench, reaching under me to pinch my nipples, rolling them between his thumb and forefinger. "I love pounding you from behind, but do miss staring at your pretty little face," he whispered into my ear, making me melt.

Latching my wrists into the cuffs, he spread my knees wide and cuffed my ankles. Now I was kneeling on the step, my torso stretched across the top like some sort of medieval offering. It was hard not to laugh, but then his hands ran along my inner thighs, and I realized that anyone could walk by and stare right between my legs.

His palms skimmed along my ass cheeks, and I tried to

calm my breathing. The first smack was perfect, right in the center of my left cheek. Hard enough to make me jump and squeal as the noise rang through the room. I couldn't help noticing a few people glance over and grin.

The spanks alternated from side to side, covering my ass, my outer thighs, my hips. I tried not to squirm, but it felt so wonderful. I felt tiny, possessed, and controlled – just the way I'd learned that I adored.

His smacks became a little harsher, and my shoulders clenched for a moment, then I tried to relax them. He noticed immediately, whispering in my ear, "I'll ease up, baby. I was just testing your reaction."

"Thank you, Master," I murmured automatically.

My head was beginning to swim as I fell into the blissful calm of subspace – energized and obedient, completely lost in the moment.

He came to the front to check my eyes carefully. "My sweet baby, do you want to please me now?"

I stretched my head up so that I could nod eagerly. "Yes, Master. Always."

His large hands glided down my spine, then over the warmed skin across my ass. His fingers dropped to my inner thighs, working up slowly.

I could feel how wet I was becoming and my tight nipples were pressing into the leather of the bench. Glancing around the room, a few people were looking in our direction now and then, but nobody was staring. Maybe they wouldn't notice us if I was quiet.

Thick fingers explored my outer pussy lips, opening me gently. I tried to be still, but my back arched as my body pressed back against his hand.

"I know how much you need it, baby," he said softly. "Say it. Tell Master what you need."

I twisted my head back so that I could whisper, "If it should please you, Master, I would like you to take me now."

"So quiet," he teased. "I'm not sure I heard you, my sweet pet."

Dammit. He knew how difficult it was for me to speak up, especially with dirty talk, and especially during sex. But as a thick finger swirled around my wet inner lips, my body tightened. I needed him desperately, and my embarrassment would have to step out of the way.

"Please, Master," I whispered louder. "Take me."

He plunged his finger inside me as I felt my pussy becoming extremely wet, my juices flowing freely as my body had been trained to know what's coming next.

"Louder."

His finger slowly pulled out, leaving me feeling empty. Tied down, helpless and needy, so aroused I could have snapped, I had no choice but to give him what he wanted, what he was trying to teach me.

"Please fuck me, Master," I said in a clear, normal voice. "Your pet is empty without your cock inside her."

He seemed surprised at my words, and I heard the familiar zip of his suit pants. The sensation of his cock circling my entrance, rubbing against my clit before dipping slightly inside me… it was a feeling of both relief and anticipation at once.

As he began to press inside, opening my tight tunnel, I didn't care if anyone was watching. The electricity between us was incredible.

"Thank you, Master," I said clearly.

His hands stroked my back gently as he worked himself inside. Glancing back for a second, I could see how incredibly aroused he was. He really seemed to like this environment, and the way I was letting him control me completely.

It didn't feel like he was showing off to his friends. It was more like he was showing the two of us how deep our bond was, how complete his control and my submission ran.

Or perhaps this was also a public declaration of ownership. He was telling the room full of the most important people in the community that he owned me now. That I belonged to him.

I couldn't think anymore as he plunged deep, grabbing my hips as he took long, slow strokes. My tight pussy walls were gripping him firmly, or perhaps he was simply deeper at this angle. The pressure was incredible, and I felt myself twitching with need.

"Relax, baby," he murmured, slowing his pace. "Take a look around. Enjoy the moment."

Tipping my head up a little, I could see a few people looking over at us. From this angle, all they could see was my ass in the air, and Master standing behind me. But it was extremely obvious as to what was happening, as his hips pushed against me, and my body leaned forward on the bench.

A few people were openly staring but looked away when they saw me notice. Most people were simply glancing occasionally, content to be near such debauchery but not being so crass as to openly ogle us.

Plunging deeper, I heard myself moan, unable to stop it. Immediately his hand stroked my back. "Good girl. Just let it all go."

My muscles were on fire, and the arousal was coursing through me as he reached under to place his fingers against my clit. I needed to come so desperately that I immediately began rocking against his hand.

"Good girl," he murmured. "Come for me."

"Yes, Master," I whispered, letting the energy begin to gather in my center.

He stopped moving completely. "What was that, pet? I didn't quite hear you."

"Yes, Master," escaped my lips louder, in a moaning cry of pure need. If anyone heard me, they knew instantly that I was moments from exploding.

"That's my girl," he said gently, thrusting hard and deep while massaging my clit firmly.

The bench was placing me at the perfect angle for him to fuck me impossibly deep, and I was overwhelmed by sensation, my twat gripping him hard, greedy for every stroke. It felt like he was truly getting off on the idea of being in public. Everything felt a little more intense, and I was right on the edge.

Master buried himself inside me so deeply it made my heart race even more. But then he stopped – unfastening my ankle cuffs, pinning me against the bench with just his hands. Then he quickly unfastened my wrist cuffs.

Leaning firmly across my back, he spoke into my ear, "Sit up on the bench."

He pulled out, standing beside the bench as I carefully crawled up to sit on top of it. I was at the perfect height now to wrap my legs around his waist, as he plunged back inside me.

"Hold on to me," he commanded.

I could feel my juices dripping along his cock as he ground into me, my soft pussy stretching around him while my legs and hips tried to hold on.

Clinging to his shoulders, he possessed me completely as he rammed me quick and deep. My little cries filled the room, and the wet, slick sounds of him fucking me hard could not be mistaken for anything else.

I couldn't even look around the room, curious about how many pairs of eyes were staring, but too lost in the moment to really care. It felt like my body was trying to swallow his, stroke after stroke as he took me hard.

"Sierra," he groaned, "You want me to fill your sweet little cunt?"

I was barely seated on the bench, as he lifted me, lowering me down to slam onto his thickness over and over.

It was so intense that my heart was hammering in my ears, my entire body wound so tight I knew I was going to climax any minute.

"Yes, Master," I whispered.

"Does my gorgeous pet still need to come?" he growled into my ear. I adored when he used that tone, and was completely losing myself in his aggressive energy.

I looked up at him, needing to please him more than I've ever needed anything in my life. "Please, Master," I asked in a clear voice that I was fairly certain half of the room could hear, "May I come all over your cock for you?"

"Yes baby," he said, his eyes searing into mine as he gripped my ass roughly, ramming up into me as I moaned endlessly.

"You're so wet for me, gorgeous," he murmured, burying his thick cock even deeper while I begin to wail. "Come for me now."

I began trembling as the climax roared through me, my pussy clenching so tight around him that I couldn't believe he was thrusting even faster. My back arched, and he gripped me tightly as I squealed, shuddering hard against him.

"Thank you, Master," I moaned, clinging against him for dear life.

His eyes closed for a moment, then he stared down at me with a strange expression. Then I felt him pumping me full of his hot seed, filling me completely as I squealed again, "Oh fuck, yes, Master!"

He kissed me hard, roughly, devouring my lips as he rocked against me, both of us groaning in pleasure as we clung to each other.

Then he pulled back slightly, kissing my forehead, then my hair as he held me for a moment. He gently eased out, looking down to stare at my dripping cum-soaked pussy with his odd dark grin.

"I hope that I pleased you, Master," I whispered, looking up at him.

He kissed me gently, and in that perfect moment I knew that I had given him everything that he wanted.

*** Master Enjoys His Pet's Other First Time ***

When I called Sierra into my bedroom, I knew that I should be working on finessing certain kinds of bondage and punishment with her. But seeing as we only had five days left together of our agreed-upon month long visit, there were a few things I still wanted to check off the list.

When she came in, I stopped her before she could kneel at my feet. "Lie face down on the bed."

"Yes, Master," she whispered.

She seemed startled that I was already naked, and hard as steel. But I couldn't help it– I had decided that it was high time we tried something that we had both been thinking about.

She climbed onto the bed, looking at me strangely. Her cheeks flushed pink as she studied my shaft for a moment. As she laid down, I admired her long, lean legs, and her tight, sweet peach of an ass. My cock was absolutely aching for her, but I knew I had to go slowly.

I walk to the side of the bed so I could see her eyes. "Sierra, tell me, baby. Do you want to feel your Master's cock inside your cute little ass?"

She gasped, then nodded eagerly. She didn't seem nervous about it anymore, only excited. I grabbed the bottle of lube from the bedside table drawer, almost feeling my pulse in my ears as I knelt behind her and spread her legs.

Coating myself completely, I dripped some of the gel on my fingertips, lightly coating her tightly puckered rosebud.

Then I wiped my hands on my thighs before gently rubbing her back. Reaching under, I ran my fingernails over her nipples, scraping very slightly until I heard a little gasp.

"The thing about anal sex, my sweet pet," I said gently,

"Is relaxing completely, and remembering that you are a gorgeous dirty girl."

I placed the tip of my cock against her little asshole, but did not press inside. "Are you going to let yourself be dirty for me, my sweet pet?"

Her slim shoulders twisted as she looked up at me. A hot little grin slid across her face. "Yes, Master," she said, licking her lips at me lustily.

My cock was absolutely throbbing as I pressed against her slippery, snug entrance just a tiny bit. Sliding my hand under and between her legs, I could feel the heat of her soft pussy in my palm as I cupped her sweetness.

Her hot little body was quivering under me, but I had to control myself. Slow and steady.

Sweeping her hair aside with my free hand, I kissed the back of her neck and down her shoulder blade while working two fingers into her writhing wet cunt. She was so ready for me, so eager to please us both that the head of my cock pressed inside her of its own accord. Her little sigh was adorable, and I felt my balls heavy with raw need.

I could feel her pressing into the bed with her knees, rocking her ass back against me slightly, helping me slide deeper.

"Good girl," I murmured, pulling my fingers out of her slippery tunnel to curl them around her throbbing little nub, teasing her with tiny strokes.

A shudder ran through her, and I pressed deeper. "You like being my naughty, dirty girl, don't you baby?"

"Yes, oh yes," she gasped, leaning back against me to draw me in.

Leaning in, I growled into her ear, "Is that how a pet addresses her dominant?"

She looked back at me, her eyes wide. "I'm so sorry, Master."

I smacked both of her sweet little ass cheeks just once,

and her blissful moans filled the room.

"I knew you were a bad girl," I said, "But I thought you would at least remember your manners." Pressing my fingers against her clit harder, her hips bucked back against me as I slid deeper.

"Oh… Master…" She whispered. "It's so thick."

"Where, baby? Where is my cock so thick?" I could feel her breath beginning to increase, as I thrust deeper, my slow tentative strokes almost fully inside.

"In my ass, Master," she purred. "I can't believe your entire cock is buried in my little ass."

I pushed inside her deeply, filling her as much as I could while she moaned and squirmed beautifully. Her perfect little figure was so delicate and pale, with her tight asshole gripping my shaft. I moved my hand so that my thumb was rubbing her swollen clit while two fingers plunged inside her. Her honey gushed over my fingers as her body quivered. She rocked back against me harder, trembling as her climax gathered deep within.

The bedspread was gripped in her white knuckles, her shoulders clenched, as she shrieked, "Please… Master, may I come for you?"

"Not yet, baby."

I slowed down the pace of my thumb on her clit while pounding deeper into her hot little ass. Kissing her shoulder, the back of her neck, my teeth grazed against her flesh. Her slick pussy was gripping my fingers tightly with every stroke.

"So, my dirty little girl likes having her naughty ass fucked?"

"Yes Master," she breathed, obviously concentrating trying to stave off her climax.

"Does my baby feel how much I need to come inside her?"

"Yes, Master."

I could feel my cock swelling, desperate for release. Thumbing her clit suddenly hard and fast, I buried my cock and fingers inside her, pounding hard as I filled her over and over.

"Come for me, baby."

Her moans of pleasure became shrieks of release as she gripped me hard, quivering end spasming under me.

I could no longer control myself, driving deep into her hot, tight ass while she squirmed and moaned. My blood roared in my ears as my thick cock rammed her even deeper, the tightness incredible as I gripped her waist.

"Please, fuck me harder, Master," she suddenly screamed. "Come deep in my ass. Make me your filthy dirty girl."

Her body was shaking, positively rattling, as my orgasm thundered through me. Pounding my hot, sticky cum into her, filling her sexy little ass to the brim, I fell against her back, both of us panting.

She was still twitching as I pulled out, flopping onto my back and pulling her against me. "You're so fucking hot, baby," I moaned breathlessly, wrapping my arms around her.

Sierra's small hand pressed against the center of my chest. "Master," she breathed, but didn't say anything further.

*** SIERRA'S OTHER OTHER FIRST TIME ***

It was strange how my entire life was different now. I kept analyzing everything, to make sure that I was making the right decision. But I knew in my heart and soul that I was. I have never felt like I knew my place, or what I was doing. Now I lived in a world where I knew everything that was going on at all times. I knew what was expected of me, how to behave, and how to serve.

I had read about the joys of service, but it didn't really make sense to me until this week. I lived to serve my Master. His happiness was mine. It was so simple that it was almost easy to overlook, but by serving him, I made us both incredibly satisfied.

I have no idea how the BDSM Academy usually worked. It seemed sort of casual in that a dominant would pick a submissive, take them in for thirty days, teach them all they could, then everyone would move on. I didn't even know if staying was an option.

As much as I knew that Master had real feelings for me, I couldn't quite tell whether he wanted to keep me on as a permanent fixture in his home.

I understood that some men enjoyed their toys, but always wanted something new. Perhaps he wanted a new submissive every month. Or every six months. I really didn't know about his lifestyle and habits before I came here to his home.

I wanted to know more about him. Everything. He was the most fascinating man I've ever met. The way he controlled me was absolutely incredible, and I found myself waking up each day curious about what he might do with me next.

Giving myself completely to anything had always been a problem. I couldn't commit to the few boyfriends that I'd had, friendships didn't last. Until Master gave me a stack of books, I found it tricky to even finish a textbook.

Now that I was being controlled, my focus was laser sharp. I knew what to do, how to behave in every situation. I felt like I was becoming a whole and proper human being.

I knew on some level that if I were to leave Master's home and go back to the real world, I would retain some of these lessons, and there might be a way for me to find another Master someday. But the thought of leaving him filled me with a dread that I would never have anticipated after only knowing someone for a few weeks.

These urges may have been illogical on some levels, but they felt so perfectly right, so correct, that I couldn't deny them. I needed to stay. I wanted Master to keep me. But he already knew how I felt, so there wasn't really anything more I could do beyond being the perfect pet.

When Master called me to his room, my heart raced as always, but perhaps a bit more. Since we only technically had another few days together, I felt like he was trying to check as many things off his list as possible.

The moment I knelt at his feet, his large hand settled on top of my head. "My gorgeous pet, how are you?"

"Wonderful, thank you, Master."

"Up."

I stood up quickly, trying to appear calm.

He hugged me suddenly, throwing me off guard completely. "Sweetheart, I know I've been throwing a lot at you this week. But you've been doing brilliantly."

I instinctively wrapped my arms around his neck, pressing my body against his black button down shirt. Feeling his heat, the possessive way he held me, made me feel instantly relaxed.

He picked me up and sat me on the bed. "Today you have a choice, my little pet." I nodded, waiting.

He leaned in, carefully studying my eyes. "Do you think Chloe is sexy?"

"Yes."

"Do you think Paige is sexy?"

"Yes."

He laughed suddenly. "Paige would be your choice, definitely."

"For what, Master?"

"You said that you were interested in exploring being with a girl. Is that something you'd like to do today?"

My breath hitched in my throat and there was no way he couldn't have noticed. "Whatever pleases you, Master."

He laughed again. "No, baby. Today is all about pleasing you. And allowing me to watch, if you like, because I'm a terribly perverse man who enjoys entertainment."

Picking up his phone, he sent a quick message. "Sit on the bed, pet." I nodded, sitting on the edge of his gigantic bed.

Paige tapped on the door, entered quietly, then knelt at Master's feet. She was beautifully naked except for her small black leather collar, and a tiny silver star clip pulling her hair back on one side.

"Paige, dear, our little pet Sierra has never been with a woman. She fancies you. What would you like to do with her?"

I didn't even realize that I had been openly checking her out. Her soft curves, lovely delicate skin, the way her hair tumbled over her round breasts to almost cover her nipples… she was absolutely beautiful.

"If it should please Master, I would like to make her come with my mouth and hands while Master watches."

She was so still, controlled. Speaking about having sex with me as if she were discussing a project at the office. Yet her eyes darted to mine for a split second, and the fire in that tiny glance ran up my spine like an electrical jolt.

Knowing that a woman that beautiful wanted me was a strange feeling, and I hoped that I'd be able to make her happy as well. I'd never done anything like this before, and my heart was pounding.

"I know you'll be sweet with my delicate Sierra. She's a nervous little thing, and has never been with a woman before."

Paige gave me another glance with a naughty grin, as if being my first aroused her completely.

"Pretend I'm not even here," Master said, pulling up a chair beside the bed. He settled in as if he were about to watch his favorite movie, and as much as I wanted to please him at all times, I felt like this time I should be more focused on Paige.

She rose from her knees gracefully, walked toward me, then immediately brought her lips to mine in the softest, most tender kiss I'd ever experienced. I had no idea that women kissed so differently, and was completely lost in the moment.

My fingers wrapped into the back of her hair, pulling her closer, into me completely. I crawled back onto the bed, Paige on top of me, as we scrambled up together without our lips parting. As we lay together, her hands wandered over my breasts, touching me gently, exploring my skin.

Then she nuzzled my ear, whispering, "Are you doing this for Master, or do you really want to play with me?"

"I… I want you," I breathed, pulling her lips back to mine again.

Her hand skimmed over my stomach, reaching the top of my mound just as I found the courage to cup her lovely breasts, massaging them gently. She smiled. "I like the way you touch me," she breathed, as her fingers glided along my folds as I spread my thighs slightly for her.

She pulled back, asking quietly, "Sierra, would you like me to lick your pretty little clit until you come?"

I nodded, unable to speak. Paige grinned, kissing me again, her tongue slipping into my mouth to dance with mine. I didn't even realize that I had pulled her on top of me, our breasts pressing together, our hips grinding as we both moaned softly.

Her hand glided down my side, then her lips were circling my nipple, gently sucking as my head fell back in a low moan. My fingers gripped the back of her neck, tangled in her hair as she worked her way lower, kissing along my stomach as it fluttered under her lips.

Pressing on my hip bones, I felt like my entire body was opening for her. I was her toy. I had completely forgotten for a moment that Master was watching us, but I didn't even look over to where he was sitting, presumably admiring the view. How decadent that he had his own live sex show for his amusement. But more importantly, I knew that he wanted to be involved with all of my new experiences, to be part of my sexual and submissive development.

Paige's fingers caressed the crease where my thighs became my pussy, and I gasped as she slowly, teasingly worked her way inward. Her thumbs ran along my vulva, spreading me open soft as a flower under her touch. My entire body was twitching with desire and I could feel my juices flowing already.

She dipped a finger around my inner lips, looking up at me with a grin. "I love that you're wet for me," she murmured, then she leaned in, giving the entrance to my excited pussy a deep, sensual french kiss.

My gasp of shock was overly loud, but I couldn't control it. Her fingers were spreading me so wide, her mouth had me utterly captured. It almost felt like bondage, the way she held me in place for her. Her breath was hot against my delicate skin as she opened me completely.

"What a gorgeous soft little pussy," she murmured.

She dug right in, lapping at my juices as her quick tongue darted along my slit. Her hands were gripping my upper thighs, her thumbs up holding open my outer folds, and the odd restraint was driving me crazy.

She looked up to meet my eyes, giving me a little wink. "You're delicious," she grinned.

Her tongue stroked all the way through my slit, upward to connect with my throbbing little button. I gasped, trying to stay still while my body needed to squirm. She bathed my inner cunt with her luscious tongue, then I felt her finger gently easing into my wet tunnel.

She was being both gentle and bold, and her completely unique energy was incredibly sensual. It was fascinating how different a woman's touch was, and I found myself lost in a sea of pure sensation. I wasn't trying to impress her or please her, just feel with her.

She added a second finger, plunging inside me deeply, gently, while making a slight swirling motion so that she was connecting with every single nerve through every stroke.

My fingers wrapped into her hair as I pulled her deep, moaning shamelessly. She alternated between licking my clit and sucking along the edges of my pussy lips, my entire body on fire as she seemed to cover my entire cunt with her mouth.

It was so intimate, doing this with someone I barely knew. But it didn't matter. My body was somehow responding in a slightly different way, where the physical was much more important than the mental trip.

My belly began to flutter deep inside, in that familiar way while my muscles began to quiver and stiffen. I felt like I was being drawn to the edge of a cliff, not quite knowing when I was going to tumble over it.

"Yes," I breathed, "Oh my... I..." Words were failing me, and my gasps and moans were too loud.

Her tongue flattened against my clit, rubbing upward sharply in steady strokes as she fucked me deeply with her hand. Paige's gorgeous eyes looked up at me, sparkling in delight as she knew I was about to come any moment.

The warmth washed over me slowly, dreamily, then spiked, leaving me squealing, writhing, as intense waves of pure pleasure pulled me apart from within.

When I finally stopped gasping, Paige came up to lie on top of me, kissing me deeply with my honey still on her lips. My hands gripped her shoulders, our bodies moving as one as we lazily groped each other.

She flipped over, pulling me on top, still kissing me, our breath and lips sealed together as if we never wanted it to stop.

But I was overcome with curiosity. Slipping lower, I gently wrapped my lips around her nipple while caressing her soft breasts gently. It was interesting, knowing pretty much what it felt like from the receiving end.

She seemed to enjoy it, giggling as I kissed a trail from one side to the other, pulling her other nipple between my lips and sucking gently while stroking her sensitive skin. The tiniest moan escaped her throat, and I was oddly proud.

I had no idea if I would be good at this, but I was so excited to try. Moving farther down, I kissed along her ribs, her stomach, working my way between her legs. She spread her slim thighs excitedly, and I let my fingers wander all along her skin, exploring every fold. Slowly I studied every crevice, taking my time.

Glancing up at her, she was smiling, obviously enjoying my attention.

Extending my tongue, I began lapping along her outer pussy lips, loving her little sigh of satisfaction. Placing a finger at her entrance, I circled gently, barely dipping in to moisten it. Knowing that I was making her wet drove me wild, and my lips wrapped around her clit as I slowly circled faster, teasing her a little.

Her fingers danced along my shoulders, which I assumed was meant as encouragement.

Flickering my tongue against her swollen button, the texture of her skin there was fascinating. It seemed so sensitive, raw, needy. It was arousing me as I steadily licked her, adoring her little moans.

Finally I plunged a finger inside, and she gasped while clutching my hair. Feeling an odd surge of satisfaction, I added a second finger, fucking her as deeply as my hand would allow.

It certainly seemed like I was hitting all of her buttons just right, as her low moans gathered strength, her back arching slightly as she rocked against my tongue. I placed my free hand at the top of her mound, pulling her skin up slightly with my thumb to expose her clit more as I clicked across the entire surface steadily.

"Yes," she gasped, "Oh… Sierra – don't stop."

I dug in, adding a third finger as I felt her tunnel walls beginning to convulse. Increasing my pace very slightly, fucking her harder, deeper. She began to wail, clutching me as her juices flowed freely, coming on my tongue as she writhed under me.

She slowly simmered down, falling back against the bed with a satisfied sigh. "Wow. That was… wow."

I laid beside her, giving her a soft, slow kiss, then snuggling against her. We laid together for a moment, then suddenly I remembered that Master was watching us.

I glanced over to see him positively beaming.

I knew that Paige was his submissive, his assistant. Occasionally they had sex but it wasn't a regular thing, and she had other lovers. But I could tell that he obviously cared for her. As he watched us curled up together, catching our breath, his eyes were filled with absolute delight.

"Master," Paige murmured, "I hope you are pleased."

"Yes, my pets," he said, watching me grin at him. "That was a vision I shall cherish forever."

Paige gave me a little squeeze. "You're incredibly sexy,

Sierra. I hope that we can play again."

I nodded, suddenly shy and not sure what to say. She smiled at me, and I kissed her cheek. "That was amazing," I whispered.

She snuggled me closer, moving her lips to my ear. "He's going to need to fuck the blazes out of you now," she breathed. "You're in for an amazing time."

She giggled, leaning back, and I saw that Master raised an eyebrow curiously, but didn't ask.

"Master, should I go back to the office so that you have some time with your primary pet?"

I felt the strangest little thrill as she said that, but couldn't put my finger on why.

"Yes, thank you, Paige," he said.

She got up, going over to where he sat and giving him a little kiss on the cheek. Turning back to wink at me, she said, "See you soon, Sierra," as she left, closing the door behind her.

I rolled toward Master, sprawled across his bed, likely wearing a giant dopey grin. He was smiling at me, not moving.

"Well, baby, how do you feel?"

"Like my body was dipped in valium, Master," I laughed. "That was… something."

He laughed with me, his low rumble filling the room. "I love it when you're all sex-high, my sweet little pet."

Kicking off his shoes and socks before he stood up, he began unbuttoning his shirt. "You've likely had enough for today, baby. We should go to sleep."

I rolled onto my elbows, propping myself up so that he could see my breasts, and my ass thrust in the air. Sticking out my bottom lip dramatically, I whined, "I don't wanna go to sleep, Master."

He laughed as he threw his shirt aside, then stepped out of his pants and shorts.

"I like it when you're naked with me, Master," I said as he climbed onto the bed, his muscular chest suddenly taking up most of my vision.

Pushing him onto his back, I was instantly on top of him, kissing him roughly as I rubbed my wet pussy against his almost-hard shaft. My hands pressed against his pecs as I wriggled against his cock.

"Do you need to fuck me, Master? Did watching your little girl with her mouth full of pussy turn you on?"

His pupils were wide, enjoying my sudden aggression. I couldn't help myself. I felt like my heart was racing from too much adrenaline, and I needed him to take me hard and wear me out.

"Yes, that aroused me more than I expected," he said honestly. "I adore watching you climax, Sierra. I think it's my favorite thing in the whole world."

That startled me. I reached down to maneuver his cock so that it was lying flat under my wet pussy lips. Rocking up and down his length, I didn't know why I was teasing myself instead of just ramming him inside me, but it felt so good. Feeling his hot, hard shaft rubbing against my now oversensitive clit was driving us both wild.

I kissed him, our wet tongues devouring each other, then I suddenly giggled. "Do you like it when I taste like Paige, Master?"

"I like you every possible way, my baby," he murmured, nibbling along the side of my throat as I straddled him, tilting so that his thick head was nestled right between my soaking, open pussy lips. I squirmed, sinking him inside me as his hands stroked my back gently.

We both groaned at the slow, steady pressure. Feeling him fill me was always perfect, and I hoped that it was something I could experience every day for the rest of my life. His lips lowered to my breasts, kissing across my skin gently as his hands gripped my ass, helping me rock up and down slowly as I opened for him.

As his shaft finally bottomed out inside me, he held me still. "Baby, did you enjoy your time with Paige? Was that everything you were hoping for?"

I grinned. "Yes, Master. That was different than what I expected. More intense. And odd with someone I don't know. But amazing."

He laughed, thrusting up into me slowly, deeply. "You didn't know me at first."

I nodded, opening my legs a little wider so there was more pressure when he hit the end of my tunnel. I loved it when he overwhelmed me completely.

I loved that he wasn't jealous at all, sharing me with a girl. And I loved the way our bodies felt like they were made for each other. He gripped my ass more roughly, grinding deep as the head of his cock kissed the end of my tunnel with every stroke. Feeling him so full and thick inside me was somehow thrilling and comforting at the same time.

"You like that, don't you, pet?" he growled softly. "When I fill your tight little pussy completely."

"Yes, Master," I breathed, pressing my palms against his chest as I wriggled my hips. "Your cock belongs inside me. Every day, for as long as you like. My body is here to please you, Master."

My own pleasure was building, and I was getting close as my climax built steadily. His hands released my ass, cupping my breasts firmly as he began to twist my nipples, massaging them against his thumb and forefinger while I moaned.

It felt like I couldn't quite breathe fully, my body was so tight – right on the edge. "May I come, Master?" I begged, my voice a little higher from the tension in my core.

"I will never get tired of hearing you beg for me, baby," he growled, and the look in his eyes as he locked with mine was more intense than I had expected.

Lexie Renard

But it wasn't an answer. I assumed that he needed to hear more. "Master, please, may your pet come for you?"

He felt so hard, so thick inside me that it was like he was stretching me open more than usual. He was kneading my breasts roughly, massaging my skin with his huge hands as he thrust up inside me. I could feel my pussy absolutely dripping, soaking both of us as I bounced up and down, right on the edge as my heart felt like it was rattling in my chest.

"Master, please let me come. Your gorgeous cock feels so perfect inside me. Don't you want to feel your little pet squeeze you even tighter?"

His eyes blazed as he watched me struggle to talk dirty for him, his lips twitching and a slight grin. My body began to quiver from the effort of holding back my climax.

"Are you mine?" he demanded in a strange, dark voice.

"Yes, Master. Completely."

"Come for me, my pet."

With three more thick strokes, my clit grinding against him, my nipples burning from his twisting and pinching, I fell over the edge. I came so hard I saw purple and teal lights flashing in front of my eyes, as the pleasure rained over me.

"Thank you… Master…" I squealed, as I rode him harder.

His hands returned to my ass, grabbing me harshly as he thrust up into me with his full strength.

"Come inside me, oh my God, yes... Please fill me, Master…" I babbled incoherently, needing the sensation of him losing himself inside me.

With a long, low groan, he blasted burst after burst of his hot seed deep in my quivering pussy. I cried out, then lurched forward to kiss him, our passion searing our lips together.

After we came down from our ridiculous high, he rolled me to the side, tucking me against his chest. "Mine," he murmured, kissing my forehead.

At that moment I realized there was a very real chance of him keeping me, and my heart raced all over again.

*** MASTER'S LESSONS ***

Although I had done almost everything I could think of with Sierra during her almost month-long stay with me, I always came back to the basics. Watching her luscious figure tied up my bed, naked and writhing, my little toy to play with – it always drove me crazy.

I had trained many girls during my time with the BDSM Academy, and always felt a sense of wistfulness when it was time for them to leave. Most of them seemed to see this month as a sabbatical or vacation. An escape from their regular lives, where they learn and grow and take these lessons with them forever.

But very few people are suited to the twenty-four seven immersive lifestyle as a permanent way of life. Most people don't do well in isolation. Most people who wish to be controlled only truly want that for several hours a day.

I was running out of our official time together, and although I desperately wanted to keep her, I needed her to say it again. We had only been together for two weeks or so when she said she wanted to stay with me, and I wasn't sure if she was high on adrenaline at the time. I was fairly certain that she was completely serious, but wanted to make sure.

I needed to be certain that it was her own desire, not a deep-seated need to please her Master.

I knew that I should be much more strict with where I drew the lines between us, but she was so irresistible I was losing control. It was hard not to think of her as a girlfriend, as a relationship. We had just been spending so much time together that it felt so natural. But I was supposed to be the one in charge.

When I called for her, she came into my room with the cutest little smile, as if she could not wait to see what we would be up to next. The second she saw that I was already naked, I noticed her nipples harden into little peaks.

It thrilled me that her body was so in tune that she became aroused by just the anticipation of what was to come.

"On your knees on the bed," I said quickly, before she even had a chance to kneel.

I pulled out a leather harness, and her smile lit up the room. She was getting more fascinated with bondage, and seemed to take it as a personal challenge.

Slowly wrapping the leather strips around her soft skin, I buckled her chest in snuggly, then wound wider strips around her waist and the top of her thighs. Binding her ankles to just below her cute little bum, and her wrists behind her back, she was standing on her knees while I held her up, completely restrained.

"Does anything pinch or pull?" I asked, checking the tension on every place where she would be bearing weight.

"No, Master. This is surprisingly comfortable."

Pulling the chains down from the ceiling, I latched her in so that she was suspended from two D-rings at her shoulder blades, and two at her hips. Using the remote control, I raised her up so that she was just a few inches off the bed.

"Still comfy?" She nodded and grinned, obviously incredibly curious.

I elevated her more so that she was a foot and a half off the bed. Grabbing a pillow, I placed my head between her legs, as she spread her knees wide. Lifting her butt up a little higher, she was slightly pitched forward. Then I lowered her a pinch at a time until her lovely soft pussy was almost brushing my mouth.

Extending my tongue, I lapped at her clit for a moment, while she squirmed and tried not to giggle. Once I got the positioning perfect, I gave her thighs a tiny push so that she was swaying gently back and forth over my tongue.

"Oh, oh…" she moaned. Looking up at her beautiful face, she looked completely overwhelmed already.

Extending my tongue farther, her swaying steadied so that she was receiving a butterfly-soft lick with every pass over my mouth. Her eyes were wide, and she was panting already.

Holding up my hand, I gave her a thumbs up and thumbs down signal to ask her if she liked it.

"This is amazing, Master. But it…"

Her hips bucked involuntarily, and it looked like she was twitching deep inside. Lowering her a pinch, I steadied her, sucking her swollen clit into my mouth.

"Master… I…"

Ramming my tongue deeply into her hot little cunt, I fucked her with it while she squealed. I could feel her entire body quaking, and was delighted at how unbelievably responsive she was.

"Does my beautiful pet need to come on my tongue?" I murmured, lapping up her sweet juices then returning to her clit.

"Yes, Master. May I?"

"Not yet, my darling."

Raising her up again, I restarted her gentle swing rhythm, pressing my tongue against her desperate button while she swung over it. I could almost feel the wave of pure arousal washing through her, as her hot little body quivered above me.

Running my fingertips gently along her thighs, her ass, I needed to feel her explode in my mouth like an overripe peach.

"Master, please," she whined, her hips shaking with need.

Lapping at her hot little clit mercilessly, I knew it was a bit nasty to torment her like this, but I could not resist. Delaying her pleasure increased mine on a level I could not even quite understand.

I knew she loved being restrained. I knew she loved

strange sexual positions and sensations. But the way she was going absolutely wild from this made it instantly one of my favorite games.

The slow deliberate rhythm of my licking seemed to be driving her insane, and making my sweet pet this aroused was a pleasure beyond sex. It felt like her body was on fire, and I could hear that her breathing was becoming more ragged.

"If you are truly mine, if I own you completely, my pet, come hard for me now."

I extended my tongue, flattening it against her sensitive clit while she rocked against me, her hips grinding into me in the air as she screamed, "I'm yours, Master," just as I slid two fingers deep into her gushing pussy.

I don't think I've ever seen her come so hard, twitching and crying out as her eyes burned into mine. Her body flailed, even though restrained, and the trembling seemed to rumble through her for longer than usual.

*** SIERRA'S INVITATION ***

I couldn't breathe, couldn't see, couldn't mentally process how intense that climax was, but I felt myself descending.

He lowered me completely so that I was lying on my side, the pressure completely off my body. Even though I hadn't been suspended for very long, I appreciated how careful he was with me.

His quick fingers undid the straps around my legs, laying me out straight, then untying my chest harness. Shoving everything away, he let me lie flat on my back.

I answered before he asked. "Thank you, Master. Everything feels fine."

He laid beside me, resting his hand on my stomach, letting me relax and breathe for a few minutes. "Do you enjoy the sensation of being restrained, little one?"

"Yes, Master."

"Why? Please, speak freely."

"There are many reasons. I like that you surprise me. You're sometimes very creative with your restraints, like today." I couldn't help giggling. "I really felt like a toy when you were controlling me like that."

"Go on."

"It's… easier to lose myself completely. I know that I belong to you, that I'm your toy. But when I'm helpless and you're controlling my every move, it's more intense, Master."

He pulled me into his arms, kissing me gently for a moment. "I love having you as my toy."

Smiling up at him, I hoped he could see in my eyes all of the things I couldn't say. His soft, gentle kiss became more heated, and I felt everything begin to stir again in both of us.

Rolling us carefully, he was above me, my legs

spreading for him as his shaft automatically searched for where I needed him.

Something felt different. There was no possession, no aggression. His thick cock pressed gently into my snug, wet pussy so naturally. I released a soft sigh as he entered me, and I could feel his shoulders twitch slightly under my hands.

"I love the way you feel inside me," I moaned into his ear. I didn't even realize for a moment that I hadn't addressed him properly, but he didn't seem to care.

"You feel so perfect, my baby," he murmured, his lips moving down my throat to suck gently at my nipples. My hands slid into his hair, pulling him against me.

"Yes," I whispered. "More."

His shaft bottomed out inside me, filling me completely, as we both sighed in relief as if we'd been needing it desperately. His long, slow strokes were gentle, controlled, and his hand scooped under my shoulders to hold me against him.

"You have the most luscious body, my sweet baby," he moaned, "But your sweet, clever mind is even sexier."

"I love the way you touch me," I murmured. "The way you read me so perfectly." My legs wrapped around his waist, pulling him deeper as my hips rocked up against him.

I realized with surprise that this wasn't a Master taking his submissive. This was a man and woman in love, enjoying each other, expressing their desire physically. At least, that's what it felt like to me.

He felt my little tremor of shock and kissed my forehead. "I know, baby. Shh, I know."

Claiming my lips again, he moved against me, his hips driving him deep and slow. Without even thinking, I reached down to spread my pussy lips so that he was pressing harder against my clit with each stroke.

Just a few weeks ago I was too shy to touch myself

in front of a man, but now I felt like I could have done anything in front of him, with him, to him.

I felt my entire pussy hugging his thickness like a caress, and he seemed to be kissing me deep within with every stroke.

I'd never experienced this before. The feeling of making love was totally overpowering, and the fire building in my belly felt like it would burn me to ashes when I released it. Looking up into his deep eyes, I could see that he was feeling it too.

We melted into each other, hands caressing shoulders, hair, exploring as we rocked as one. I kissed his throat, stroking his earlobe between my fingertips. He nibbled along my collarbone, making me gasp. My legs hugged him against me as he pumped his perfect thickness into my dripping pussy over and over.

It felt like time had stopped, and I had no idea how long we rocked gently together, caressing and stroking and loving each other so intimately.

I felt like the tension inside me was building again, and tried to settle it down – not for him to tease me this time, but because I needed to come with him.

The feeling of his thickness became fuller, and I gripped his shoulders, looking directly into those dark eyes expectantly.

His possessive passion had me completely captured, completely owned. His thumb pulled at my bottom lip tenderly, then he kissed me with a heat that radiated through my entire body.

We didn't need words. His pace increased slightly, filling me deeply as he grazed my button with each stroke.

Gasping into his lips, he knew my body so well. His slight nod as our kiss deepened was all I needed, then I was moaning into his mouth as we feasted on each other. My orgasm started like a trickle of hot water that warmed me, then flooded me, washing through me in an exquisite rush as his own heat filled me deep inside. His low growl rumbled through my mouth as we came together, energizing each other's sensations as we both vibrated from the sweet, savage force that ran through us.

He slowed his rhythm very gradually until we clutched each other in perfect stillness. The intensity of that heat was slowly dissipating around us. Looking up at him, his tender expression nearly stopped my breath completely.

"Sierra, I know you felt that." He skimmed his fingertips across my forehead, brushing a few wisps of fallen hair from my eyes. "That was incredibly intense. How do you feel, sweetheart?"

My lips parted to begin, "I..." But no real words came. Staring up into his eyes, my insides were falling apart. I couldn't express everything that was surging through me.

He sat up, pulling me into his lap, stroking my back gently. "Tell me what you want, baby. Tell me what you need. Speak up."

His eyes were blazing as if he were trying to make me say something. As if he needed me to say the magic words, but I couldn't even think. "I want you to keep me," I blurted. "I want to stay with you."

"Yes, baby. I want you to stay," he said gently but clearly. His deep eyes were locked on mine, as I nodded.

I threw my arms around him desperately, shaking with relief. He sweetly swept his thumb under my right eye to wipe away the tear threatening to spill down my cheek.

"Sierra, if you would like to live here with me, I would love to have you. You can stay as long as you like, and leave at any time. We'll have a weekly meeting to make sure both of our needs are being met, and I swear I will care for you completely."

"Thank you, Master," I whispered, my throat tight.

"I can send an assistant and movers to your apartment

to help you pack. You're welcome to bring as much as you like, or we can put things in storage at one of my other properties."

My hair swayed across his chest as my head tilted, processing. "Master, are you rich?" I blurted out, instantly embarrassed.

He laughed. "I'm quite comfortable, yes."

I couldn't help giggling. "I didn't know if this house belonged to you, or if maybe you borrowed it for when you taught a submissive, or something."

"No, this is all mine. I'll have many things to show you over the next several years, my sweet little pet." His smile lit up my heart in a way I'd never felt before.

"I hope to make you happy, Master."

"You already do, sweetheart." I realized that I was leaving my entire life to be with him, and he seemed to understand how precious that was. He pulled me to the edge of the bed, then he stood up.

I felt so tiny sitting before him, and was absolutely shocked when he fell to his knees in front of me, taking my hands in his. "I love you, Sierra." My mouth fell open in shock as he quickly continued, "I know that it's only been a month, but I feel like I've been searching for you my entire life. I…"

I leaped forward, throwing him backward so that I was lying on top of him on the floor. "I love you, Master," I gasped before kissing him with my entire body, wrapping around him as our skin melted together, his hands gripping my back gently, yet possessively. I knew at that moment that I was his completely. Forever.

***

***

Continue the BDSM Training School series with
Preparing Emma (Book #4)
Examining Hanna (Book #7)
Taunting Rachel (Book #10)
Each girl has three books of submissive exploration.

***

**Comedy, Sci-Fi, Romance, and delicious sensual smut...
Get on the email list at LexieRenard.com for updates and monthly free ebooks!**

HOT, EROTIC STORIES YOU MAY ENJOY:

Heights of Luxury: Dystopian Future Erotic Romance Novel
*The air, the light, the technology, the rules... everything was wildly
different 71 Levels up.* Ellie only had one goal in life – to provide for her
little sister. Decadent bachelors Adam and Ben share everything – their
business, and their luxury condo up Level 71. When Adam bought Ellie in
the Condo Courtesan Auction, he was surprised that his dark urges were
finally triggered, and Ben was shocked to discover it was a girl he'd already
seen. Will innocent Ellie be able to keep up with their unusual sensual
appetites, while following the new restrictive rules of the higher levels?
What will happen when she discovers the little secrets that both Ben and
Adam tried to hide? 18+: Many *extremely* vivid, graphic sexual scenes.

Sharing my Submissive Pet (BDSM Hotwife erotica)
If you truly love your wife, share her with a friend…
Nick adores his sexy wife Julia, who is his devoted submissive pet. But she
craves constant sex, and he's just one man. He takes her to visit a friend
who is freshly divorced, and looking for some hot action. Dave gives Julia
just what she needs (as well as fulfilling his own fantasy to spank a naughty
girl), then helps Nick try to tire the hot little vixen out thoroughly.

Billionaire's Sugar Baby: From Trailer Trash to Sex Pet (5 part series)
Grace was shivering in an alley when she met her Prince Charming. Well,
he wasn't a prince, but Cole Hawthorne was so rich and powerful in this
city it was practically the same thing. When faced with the decision to go
back to her trashy trailer park, or come home with Cole, she decides to take
a chance and move up in the world. Being Cole's secret mistress could be
the answer to all of her problems, but will she be able to satisfy him?

Please Spank Me, Master (Romance Novella) First Time BDSM
Amy's biggest crush comes into her coffee shop without seeming to notice
her, but when she peeks at Eric's laptop, she discovers that he's into BDSM.
She tiptoes into the local scene and finds out it's a way to transform her
shyness, and unleash her sensual desires. When Eric sees this new side of
Amy and wants to be her Master, will she let go and beg for what she really
wants? Or will she feel like she's going too far, too fast?

My Neighbour's Dungeon - 5 part Series BDSM Submission Romance
What does a girl have to do to get the next door neighbor to spank her?
Pretty little Lindsay has lived next to gorgeous older hunk Nick for years,
but she just accidentally discovered that he is an S&M Master. Super
romantic submission and BDSM exploration!

Carrie's Cuffs (BDSM office erotica)
A woman in complete control discovers her hidden submissive side.
Carrie ruled her entire office, and was the picture of efficiency. When
she is trapped with the hunky new intern Brad, she quickly finds that she
needs him to control her. The second she is cuffed, she becomes a different
person, completely in touch with her submissive, sensual side. Brad eases
her slowly into the idea of her being his little toy until she gives herself
completely in every way.

Tying Tracy (First time bondage BDSM erotica)
A jumpy woman finds stillness when her new boyfriend ties her down.
Tracy hates that she's so twitchy all the time. Jim wonders how she'd react
to bondage, and they quickly discover it's exactly what she needed. As
Tracy learns more about the world of BDSM, she finds that giving her body
and control to Jim allow her to feel peaceful... then more excited than she'd
ever been before.

The Sitter - BDSM House Pet: First Time Domination, Submissive
A sweet little pet to play with for the weekend...
When David asked his buddy to take care of his girlfriend Anna while he
was away for the weekend, Tyler thought he meant to check in on her in
case she needed anything. It turns out that Anna was actually a submissive
pet, and required a lot more attention than Tyler could ever have imagined.
Suddenly he was in charge of a smoking hot twenty-one year old who was
begging him for spankings, and eager to serve him in every possible way.

Suddenly His Toy - a Sexy Office Pet Romance   BDSM Erotica
The job title is "assistant", but the boss wants MUCH more from her...
Sarah is a new assistant, catching the eye of the CEO who wants to use
her as his sex pet and toy. At first she plays his games because she needs
the money, but suddenly she discovers that she's addicted to him - his
punishments, the rough, hot encounters, and the adrenaline that crashes
through her veins every time she's near him.

Coming Soon...
More hot romance novels, and tons of new erotic short stories!
LexieRenard.com for details, and get on the email list for treats.

If you enjoy sexy modern romance, search for **Whispered Curses**,
available on Kindle, Kindle Unlimited, and in Paperback.

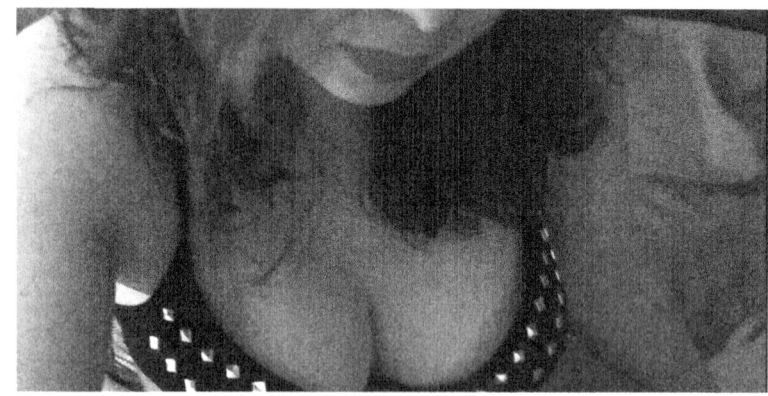

About the Author

Romance, S&M romance, erotic romance, and erotica
writer Lexie Renard is from Toronto, Ontario, and
a sketchy bar or dungeon near you.
Yes, she's actually bisexual and into the BDSM scene.
No, you may not see her wrist cuffs, you naughty thing.
If you like romantic, interesting smut, and a wide variety of
strange stories, search "Lexie Renard" on all ebook sites.
(Some sites allow filthier stories than others.)

Get on the email list for a FREE story, longer previews, and
details of new releases: http://eepurl.com/cP-J_L

www.LexieRenard.com

Want to be a hero to an author you enjoy? Review their work online.
Even if it's a super short review, it really helps increase visibility.
On most sites you can change your name to initials if you'd like
to maintain your privacy.

Thanks for being one of the cool people who still read books!

~ *Lexie xox*

Printed in Dunstable, United Kingdom

66412875R00067